The Lifetime Story of OH-Y-YEE

The Strong, Beautiful and Sassy Indian Mare

MICHAEL OSMUNDSON

The Lifetime Story of Oh-y-Yee
Copyright © 2022 by Michael Osmundson

ISBN
978-1-958122-11-2 (Paperback)
978-1-958122-12-9 (Hardcover)
 978-1-958122-10-5 (eBook)

Table of Contents

Chapter 1

High up on the mountainside stood a jasper pine tree that was so tall that it looked as though it reached heaven. It was the best-looking tree in that part of the forest, dark green in color with a bright fire-red-orange bark that was outlined in black. The contrast between the bark and the pine needles was amazing to the human eye. There was the smell of pine needles and pine cones in the air. It was also early in the spring, which just seemed to magnify the sounds and smells. It was amazing to someone else too.

He sat there high up in the tree, looking down and across the valley below. He was also looking across the valley to the mountainside opposite the big, tall tree. His eyesight was as sharp and clear as it had ever been, even though he was getting up in the years. Spotting a squirrel or a mouse running on the mountainside was very easy for him. He could pick them off very easily and have them for a meal if he wanted.

The limb he was perched on was thick and heavy and had seen many years of wear. Hie big nest next to him had raised many babies. His mate had died last winter. For fourteen seasons, they had raised their offspring in this tree. This big bald eagle was the symbol of America because of his skill as a warrior and hunter.

Just then, something sparkled from the corner of his eye, a movement. It was very small, but it was a movement. It was in the forest across the valley and about halfway up on the mountainside. There it was again, like a twinkle from a diamond. Hie eagle was now homing in on the spot where he had seen the twinkle. And then it appeared again in the small clearing.

It was a group of eight Indian warriors wearing war paint, black over white—the color of the Crow nation. They had a sign of a hand on the right side of their face within a large circle of white and their favorite weapon on the left. Hie meaning behind the paint was this: "We will put our hand on your face, and with the other, we will kill." The Crow were the worst enemy you could have from the Mississippi River on the east to the Pacific Ocean on the west. Torture was their favorite way of eliminating the enemy. Their horses also carried war paint with circles around their eyes and the hand on their rump. They had feathers tied into their manes and tails. The group was moving as though they had already spotted the target. Sweat was running off the horses, and they looked tired, but on they continued through the bushes and back into the trees. Now they were out of sight.

The Crow in the lead was riding a big, tall, and strong female horse dapple-gray in color, darker in the front than the rear with a solid black mane and tail. She was a beauty and very impressive like she should be ridden by a general in the army. This mare had war paint on her head and rump. She had a circle of white paint around her left eye and the dreaded hand on her rump. This war party was moving very fast through the woods. The horses were sweating and short of breath like they had been traveling fast for some time now. Oh- y-Yee was her name, which in Crow meant "strong mountain."

The warriors were not talking but only using sign. The quivers were full of newly made arrows. Beef jerky hung from their waistband. They were traveling light, nothing extra.

Oh-y-Yee was getting a little upset with her rider as he continued to kick her in the ribs, trying to prompt her to go faster. She was traveling fast enough, and that was all there was to it. She was not going to put up with this much longer, and she knew how to stop it for good. Oh-y-Yee was not a stranger to her rider, who had captured her five years before in a dead-end canyon. She thought she was going to escape that day, but she stepped in a gopher hole and twisted her ankle just before the escape was possible. He jumped on her, and to her surprise, she could not throw him off. Now all she had to do was look for a low-hanging limb and buck him off.

He was also tall and strong with rough features that made him handsome in some ways. He was dark skinned and had coal black hair, which was just as black and straight as the hair of Oh-y-Yee. His muscle tone was that of a man who had worked hard and fast just to keep himself in shape. He wore a loin cloth, war paint, and a quiver of arrows along with his favorite hunting knife. War paint made him look scary and someone whom you did not want to meet in battle. His name was Awanatu, which in Miwok meant "slow turtle." He received this name from his mother, who was captured by the Crow on one of their trips west. She named him Slow Turtle because, as a boy, he was big and slow. Now he was anything but big and slow.

Awanatu had been with many raiding parties and had been so successful that he had risen to the third most powerful position in the tribe. He was feared throughout all the Plains as the brave who would kill first and ask later. Many scalps hung on his lodgepole. Awanatu had the privilege to wear three painted white dots on his forehead to show his position in the tribe. His dream was to do something great in battle so that he could gain a great chieftain's name like his grandfather, Bad Ax.

The eagle was sitting high up on the mountain, on the huge limb of the big pine tree, when another twinkle caught his eye far off in the valley below and then another and another. It was very bright, quick, and often. The eagle lifted off to check out the twinkle; maybe it was another meal or at least interesting. He glided downward toward the valley below, letting the hot air currents lift him and drop him every seventy-five feet. Now the eagle reached the valley and started to fly toward the twinkle in the far eastern end of the valley. It was hot enough down here with the sunshine on the sand and rocks, which made it almost unbearable.

As the eagle left his perch toward the valley, he noticed the Crow war party was resting their horses near a small mountain stream while they were eating some jerky. The eagle kept flying toward the second twinkle, which was much farther than he expected from the limb high in the pine tree on the mountainside. On his flight, he had saw that the landscape was changing gradually from a high desert to more of a pasture with a few deer and other animals grazing here and there. He also saw where the stream emptied into the valley from where the Crow had been camped.

Flying was always fun on hot days when the wind currents would lift you several hundred feet just because you were in its path. The eagle was playing the currents as he rounded a bend about twenty miles from his perch in the big pine tree when he saw the twinkle again. This time, he zeroed in on it, but it was another ten miles or so, so he could not make out what it was. He started to fly harder and faster to examine what that twinkle was.

Ten miles down the valley on the east end was that twinkle. It was a fine necklace made from handcrafted silver with a beautiful locket hanging from the chain. The locket was fashioned to have a picture on the inside of it, and that it had. The picture was of a little boy who was the firstborn son of Peter and Anna Peterson. He had died shortly after the picture was taken from a new illness called smallpox. That was when Peter and Anna decided to leave their home in northeast Iowa and head west. They loved Iowa and thought they would live there for the rest of their lives, but the death of Peter Jr. was more than Anna could bear, so they headed west. To where, they did not know. This little valley was somewhat intriguing during the last three days, but now it was starting to look more like a dry, arid climate. They had decided to push on from here to somewhere in the eastern part of Utah.

Peter had talked some of their friends into moving west with them. It took some time and a lot of talking to convince them, but he did. They were all of Norwegian descent—the Andersons, the Olsons, the Amdahls, the Johnsons, the Johnstons, the Jonesburgs, and the Larsons. They had made a nice little wagon train that took its time and enjoyed each day one at a time. Peter was in charge, and Mr. Anderson was the co-captain, with Ole Olson as the hunter and provider of the cooked meat when they were lucky enough to have it. They had several run-ins with Indians, mainly the Cheyenne and the Ute, but nothing major.

Peter carried a Colt .45 along with the best rifle he had ever seen, which was the 1861 Henry long barrel. It kicked like a mule when fired, but it packed a punch that no one ever wanted repeated. Where it entered, there was a hole the size of a dime, and the exit wound was huge, the size of a cantaloupe. Most of the time, no one lived after being hit directly. Most of the other men carried six-shooters of one brand or another, claiming they had the best one, and most of them had a rifle or a shotgun. The favorite was a shotgun filled with sixteen penny nails. It was like a big hand grenade.

The eagle arrived and was high in the sky above the wagon train, unnoticed. He could feel as well as see that trouble was coming their way.

With the wagon train heading west and the Crow heading east, something was about to explode.

The eagle continued to enjoy the up and down drafts from the hot weather and the heat from below. He saw the weary travelers down below, some on horses, some walking, some on mules, and the rest on the wagons. Oxen were pulling the heavy big wagons loaded with everything that they owned and sometimes too much stuff. They would have to unload half a wagonload, pull it through the slew, unload it, go back with the empty wagon, and pick up the other half of the stuff. It was time consuming. The same routine was followed when they came to a steep hill or a river to cross, and sometimes they would need two teams of horses in the front for power and one team at the back to be a brake when going downhill. They did not seem to mind the extra work because they had heard land was in the west just for the taking. It lulled them into a false sense of security.

Then the eagle decided to fly west and see if anything was developing with the Crow Indians. Evening was coming soon, so Peter decided they had gone far enough for one day, and he started looking for a good safe place to make camp. He wanted to change his site to one that had some dry wood close by instead of a half mile away. Water was also important, so he started having the wagons drift closer to the side of the valley by the stream.

The sun was blinding them now as it was setting in the west, and he thought it would be a perfect time for Indians to attack. Then Peter remembered an old-timer saying that the Indians never wanted battle at night. They were afraid of the evil spirits, so he felt more at peace with his decision. They came to a slight bend in the stream, and on the south side of the stream was a slight elevation in the land, maybe three or four feet higher, almost like someone had leveled it to build a house on it. The circle of wagons would fit on this elevation, and at the edge of it lay five trees. It looked like they had been uprooted in a violent windstorm some time ago, for they were very dry, the kind you wanted to find when camping. Peter decided that this was the spot, so he called for everyone to circle the wagons.

Now the hard work started—washing the horses in the stream, finding and cutting firewood, gathering rocks for the firepit, putting the harnesses away so that they could dry in the proper shape, tying a line and securing it between trees to tie the horses up for the night while others were hobbled so that they could graze. Someone had to milk the cow; someone had to feed the horses some hay or grass, which had to be cut; someone had to get some fresh meat; someone had to roast it. Everyone was so busy that no one thought of the dangers in this part of the world, not even once.

The eagle had made a pass over where he had last seen the Crow party. They were still there, and it looked like they were resting and were planning on doing it for a while. Their horses were grazing with hobbles on, and the Crow Indians were sitting by the fire, eating roasted deer meat, and laughing. He thought he would make a final pass over the Norwegian group to see where they were and if it was well with them. When he flew over the settlers, he could see they were sitting around the fire, eating, laughing, and telling stories. He thought of how wonderful the life of the Indians and the settlers was, when all they needed to do was feed themselves and care for the young.

With that thought, he decided to fly home tonight to the tall pine tree at the top of the mountain, where he too could rest. On the way home, he would look for something to eat. An hour later, he landed on his nest, his stomach full, and he was tired. He dozed off for the night. Tomorrow would be another day.

Chapter 2

Peter Peterson had finished his work for the day when he sat down by the campfire and ate his evening meal. It was good considering the fact that they had eaten stew for nearly every meal in the last month. Now he was very tired and decided to turn in for the night. Pete, as Anna called him, was lying under their wagon with his head resting on the soft old saddle his father had given him nearly twenty years ago. It was a warm night with a full moon shining brightly over the valley and the surrounding mountainside.

As he lay there, he couldn't go to sleep because he kept thinking about the countryside around them. It was becoming more like a desert with each day of travel, and he was thinking that maybe they should have stopped a week ago in that little green valley at the Colorado and Utah border. It looked a lot like home. But then Pete decided it was too late to worry about that, so instead, he concentrated on finding the perfect spot somewhere in the near future. He could see the toll this trip was taking on everyone in the group. And he was their leader, the man responsible.

Fifteen miles away, the Crow raiding party was sound asleep except Awanatu. He was tossing and turning, thinking about the upcoming battle with the little wagon train. The Indian scout had hurried into camp four days ago, proclaiming that more palefaces were coming through the forbidden holy land of the Crow. That land was where his ancestors were now resting high off the ground in their hammocks with their most prized possessions. Anger went through his entire body as he thought of the day when he could make them pay for their mistake. That thought brought a smile to his face, and with that, he fell into a deep sleep. Never once did he think of the fact that the little wagon train was not aware they had traveled through sacred ground.

Oh-y-Yee was grazing peacefully in the little clearing that had a nice growth of rye and orchard grass. This was some of the best grass she had eaten in a long time. Each mouthful was very sweet and tasty, and she knew this grass was high in protein, which she would need in the days ahead. She felt very safe with the full moon shining from above, highlighting the tall, long grass. Oh-y-Yee was thinking of the last few days with the hurried trip here and then, just as suddenly, the halt. And then camp was made, and everyone rested. Maybe Awanatu wasn't such a bad guy.

High up on the mountainside in the tall old pine tree sat the eagle. He couldn't sleep either as the bright moonlight was bothering his eyes, and he was just thinking of the things of the day—the two twinkles of light belonging to two different groups of humans and the fact that both seemed motivated to do something quickly. *What could be the motivator for each of them?* he wondered as he too fell asleep.

Down on the valley floor was an entirely different scene. Deer were grazing, the mountain lion was out hunting, the wolves were doing the same, plus some howling here and there just to locate one another. Once in a while, the screeching of a hoot owl could be heard far off in the distance. Overall, it was a peaceful scene that held an eerie feeling underneath your skin. The stream near the wagon campsite was singing as the water raced downhill, hitting all the rocks and limbs that lay in its way. The campfire was still blazing away, and you could hear the crackling as the logs turned into red-hot coals. Everyone and everything seemed to be in its proper place, doing what was normal.

At 3:00 a.m., everything had settled down and was really quiet. The eerie feeling was back and stronger than ever. That feeling was haunting Pete while he was sleeping, and suddenly, he was wide awake and sitting up, half scared to death. He realized he had been dreaming, and something had suddenly startled him awake. Pete lay still for a moment, hardly breathing and listening intently, when he realized that he had been startled by the loud snoring coming from under the wagon of Ole Olson. What a relief!

The morning sun was coming up in the east, and everyone could feel its heat and knew that today was going to be hot, maybe very hot. There was not a cloud in the sky when Anna awoke. She was the first one awake in her camp, and her thoughts went immediately to Peter Jr., which was normal now. Anna remembered how sweet he was and good looking too. She wondered how tall he would have been, if he would look like his father or one of his grandfathers, what his voice would sound like, or if they would still be in Iowa if he had been alive.

Anna went down to the stream to gather some fresh water for drinking and cooking. That was when it happened. She reached up and touched her necklace as she said a prayer, and it sent off another twinkle of light. The twinkle was spotted by the eagle high up on the mountain in the big pine tree. He knew they were awake at the campsite, so he decided to fly by and see what was happening today. He left his perch and started flying to the east toward the wagon train.

Overhead and looking down, he saw that the Crow war party was also awake, moving slowly around the campsite. The horses were still out in the meadow, which meant they were not leaving the campsite soon. After a few more minutes, the eagle was flying over the settlers and saw that they too were awake and moving around. They were putting the harnesses on the big workhorses, mostly Belgians. They were large horses that could work hard all day long, day after day, without losing much weight.

Pete had saddled his horse and left the campsite soon after Anna had gone to the stream. It hurt him deep inside to see his wife suffer day after day at the loss of their first son, Peter Jr. He had learned how to deal with it himself, but he did not know how to help Anna. He just worked harder and longer until he was very tired; then and only then could he sleep soundly. Pete would hear Anna crying most nights after she thought that Pete was sleeping. All the hugs and comforting words only lasted a few moments, and then it all started over again for her.

Suddenly, Pete realized he had better quit daydreaming and pay attention to details. He was about five miles out in front of the wagon train, looking for a safe way through the valley and a clear path through the mountains. He thought he had seen a twinkle of light off to the right about halfway up the mountainside, but after watching that spot for some time, he did not see it again.

Awanatu had been watching Pete for quite a long time before Pete stopped and looked directly at him. He slowly reached up and covered his bear claw necklace so that it would not twinkle in the sunlight. Awanatu stood perfectly still for what seemed like an hour before Pete started to move again. He knew that he needed to be much more careful during the next few days. This twinkle could have ruined his chance to avenge the violation of his ancestors' death site. He was confused about why the paleface was this far away from the rest of the group. Didn't he know this was the land of the Crow, the most hostile of all Indians? Awanatu thought this might be easier than planned.

Suddenly, Pete put his 1861 Henry to his shoulder and squeezed the trigger. What happened next was startling to many. The settlers way back in the valley could hear the roar of the big rifle and wondered what had happened. Ole Olson said, "If we heard another shot, Pete would be in trouble. But if not, he is most likely hunting."

Awanatu was so surprised that he just about fell down in shock as he had never in his life seen or heard a paleface fire a stick that loud. Then he saw a big buck deer fall to the ground instantly. And that was not the only surprise for Awanatu; it was the distance of the shot, which was well over seven hundred feet. He knew now that he needed a new plan, or he too would visit the sacred, holy ground himself.

Pete started to skin the deer without even knowing he had been in danger. He was cutting up all the good cuts and packing them on his horse when he thought more about it. He would just continue the butchering, and the wagon train would come to him, so he did not have to leave any meat behind or chance the fact that someone might steal it, animal or human. When Pete finished butchering, he found a nice shady spot to rest. The wagon train should be here soon, so he decided to clean the big Henry while he waited.

Awanatu was back in the Crow camp, trying to tell them what he had seen. With this, he was having trouble because it was hard to make them understand the loud noise from the 1861 Henry. He had heard rockslides down the side of mountains and thousands of buffalo running across the prairie, but neither one of them was nearly this loud. But he did his best and then told them about how far the deer had been from the paleface when he was killed. It was impressive to say the least.

The wagon train came up the trail in about an hour and a half when Pete had finished cleaning the 1861 Henry. It was now like a brand-new rifle after a complete bore cleaning as well as a light rub of oil throughout.

Pete could see that everyone was tired and moving slower than normal. He also noticed more people riding than on other days. Tonight they would find a very good spot to make camp and then stay three or four days before moving on. They had some new deer meat to eat, and he could send Ole with one or two of the other men out hunting for more meat. Maybe they could even stay a week, and the women could make jerky. It sounded good to him; now he just had to find that perfect spot where they would be safe.

Anna was very tired as she rode in the wagon, thinking about the past four months of traveling across the Plains, the High Plains, the Rockies, and now this, the High Desert. What could possibly be next? She wondered if all this was her fault because she could not stay in their nice, comfortable home in Iowa. Anna felt hopeless and thought she might start crying when she saw Peter standing by the tall oak tree at the base of the small hill. The entire wagon train picked up the pace after someone had yelled, "There's Pete!" She felt better just knowing Pete was safe and could be riding by her side for a few hours before heading out to find another campsite. Anna was proud of him because the people in the train loved him, and his style of working with everyone was honest and upright.

Awanatu was now halfway up the mountainside, looking down at the wagon train. He had brought Wounded Elk with him to scout the wagon train. He was one of the best Indians at figuring things out like where someone was going, why, and which route they would take. They wanted this attack to be successful, and if it was to be, it also had to be a surprise. They would have plenty of work ahead.

Pete had been riding on the wagon now for several hours, sitting beside Anna, which made her feel better. They talked about many things, including camping tonight and where, when, and how long they should stay. Pete agreed with her that they should camp for a week or more so they could build up the supply of meat on board the wagons. It could be jerky, salted heavily or canned. No matter how the meat would be preserved, it would be important down the trail, especially if the landscape turned into more of an arid desert.

It was time for Pete to climb down from his seat next to Anna, mount his horse, and ride out ahead of the train to find a spot to make camp. He jumped from the wagon and found out quickly that he was stiff and sore, but he mounted Old Jim anyway, thinking the stiffness would just have to work itself out. Pete looked down to make sure the big Henry was in the scabbard, and it was.

The eagle was circling high overhead, watching the scenery below, when he noticed that the Crow war party had pulled camp. They were gone, so he decided to see where they went. He flew higher and far off in the west; he spotted a cloud of dust rising out of the forest floor. The eagle flew westward to try to outpace the war party before dark, if possible. Just before sunset, he caught up with them. The Crow were setting up camp, starting a fire, putting the horses in the little meadow nearby, and setting a couple of tepees up. The eagle found a high empty branch not far from the Crow and decided to perch there for the night.

Pete found a nice place to set up camp for a few days. It was near the stream and had dry wood from a fallen tree nearby and several big game trails leading down to the stream. The valley had a real nice meadow here that looked like it has been planted with rye and orchard grasses. *It is peaceful looking, almost like northeast Iowa,* he thought as he climbed down from Jim.

Pete was happy just from the thought of camping for a while without having to saddle up every morning and get everyone moving together. Moving together was the hardest part of his job most days, and for some reason, people just did not understand what kept people doing so. It was simple for Pete, and he said it out loud. "You start moving, and you fall in behind me and keep moving, simple enough." But some of them just could not see it and were always the cause of delays.

Hie wagon train was pulling in now, so Pete started directing them into a circle. When that was finished, he handed out work details to everyone so that camp could be set up quickly. Some were gathering firewood or water, some caring for the horses, some milking the cows, and some gathering hay or grass. It was a busy place even for the boys and girls. Tonight they would have a man placed at each end of the camp working as a watchman just in case they had reached the dreaded Crow nation lands. Several men they talked to on the trail a hundred miles back had said this was where you had to keep your scalp tight on your head, and he planned on doing just that.

Tomorrow they would start maintenance on the wagons, like removing the wheels and greasing them as well as fixing different parts on them that had been broken. On the trail, they were patched just to keep the train moving. The women would be washing clothes and processing the meat.

It was welcomed because it would be different. The horses and the cattle and oxen could rest as well as graze whenever they needed to. It was going to be great.

They made two big firepits, one at each end of the camp. They had a roaring fire in each. They had started roasting some deer meat and cooking some potatoes and carrots with onions. The smell in the camp was one of the best ever. The men were trying to figure out a system for the night watchman job so that everyone served their fair time.

When Pete and the rest of the men turned in for the night, everyone else was sleeping and having nice dreams, except the two men keeping guard. They had a warm fire and a full stomach, so they too were happy.

The two night watchmen were now thinking that it must be midnight, give or take. They had heaped the bigger logs on the fire now and had a roaring fire going, which made them feel secure too as it warmed their bodies. It was surprising to them that they would be chilled like this out here at night, and it almost started as soon as the sun went behind the mountains. Off in the distance, they could hear a mountain lion making a kill, a hoot owl hooting, and the sound of water running down the stream, hitting rocks along the way. The wind was blowing in the valley, and the sound of it going through the grass was soothing to the soul. The moon was full, and it made the night seem very safe and peaceful. Was all this a sense of false security?

Chapter 3

Many miles away, the eagle was high up in a tree, just waking up from a good long night's sleep. He was hungry and thirsty and decided to fly out and look for some breakfast. When he left the branch, he saw that the Crow party was also up and moving as they were heading west in a hurried manner. The eagle thought that this was odd; first, they came into the valley a couple of days ago in a hurry to get somewhere, and now they were leaving just as fast as they came. Strange. The eagle headed east to check out the settlers to see if they were up and moving. He would just have to eat on the run, maybe hunt while he was flying toward them.

The sun was slowly starting to rise above the valley floor when the eagle appeared overhead without being seen. He looked down and saw some movement in the camp as he scouted the area. Some of the women were over by the stream gathering water, some of the men were gathering wood for the fire, some were doing odd jobs around the campsite, and some were cleaning their rifles. Everything seemed normal to the eagle as he flew away to find his next meal.

Pete was up early, saddled Old Jim, and rode off into the valley, going southwest toward a grove of aspen trees. They stood strong and tall about a mile and a half from camp. He was wondering why they were growing in that area and thought it would be a good day to find out why. Everyone was relaxing from the hard long push west, and he was no different from the rest of the party. He was enjoying the ride so much that he had forgotten they were not in Iowa just riding around the meadow that he put cattle into every summer.

When he arrived at the grove, he discovered that it had a small natural spring in the center of it. *That's how come they are growing here, more water. It all makes sense.* Pete also noticed many game trails through the grove, which meant that this could be a great place to hunt. So he started scouting the area, looking for the perfect spot from which he could hunt. In a few minutes, he found it. A small knoll in the center of the grove gave him several directions to look for oncoming game. A few minutes later, he shot a nice buck with a huge rack on him. Pete would surprise the camp with fresh meat today.

Anna was out and about, telling everyone what was needed today and directing the people this way and that, when she thought about Pete. She wondered where he had gone so early in the morning and what he was up to today. Some of the families had started cooking, and the smell made her hunger pains increase a hundredfold; now Anna would start cooking too.

The Crow party was traveling fast through the mountains, going faster than before in a west-northwest movement. The war paint was neither on the horses nor on the braves as they continued on the trail. They were content to eat buffalo jerky while riding, thinking of the five-day ride ahead of them. It would take its toll on everyone, including the big strong horse named Oh-y-Yee.

Oh-y-Yee was traveling as fast as she could right now with Awanatu on her back. She had decided that shoving him off her back would come at a later time. If she did it now, Awanatu would have her caught by the other braves quickly. She would have to pick a much better spot and time to do this. Oh-y-Yee would have to think about this for quite some time and then catch him sleeping at the wheel. She knew this trail well as it led to the main Crow nation campsite far off in the High Desert meadow near a place they called Buffalo Run.

It was north of the big, long, and flat-topped mountains the Crow called Painted Hills. Oh-y-Yee hoped that, at the end of this trip, they could rest a few days and graze in the nice meadows near Buffalo Run. She was also wondering why Awanatu was in such a hurry.

Pete was back in camp now with some fresh deer meat, and everyone was excited about it. They were going to roast some of it right away and then make jerky from the rest of it. He thought everyone deserved this rest, and he was sure they needed it now that he saw the difference in their attitudes. *We will have to do this more often,* he thought as he was drying down Old Jim. He could even see the difference in the way the animals looked and acted. *Rest is a wonderful thing. It brings back good feelings all around in humans as well as animals.*

A bunch of the boys were playing in and near the stream, laughing, screaming, and throwing rocks and sticks at one another. Girls were playing around the wagons and helping their mothers make the jerky. The men were bringing in more firewood and piling it in certain spots just to fortify the wagon train. A few of the men were watching the cattle and oxen in the meadow to keep them safe and prevent them from walking away from the herd and getting lost. Others were processing the deer hide to make a nice jacket or blanket for someone. Some of them were just relaxing in the shade, enjoying the rest.

The eagle was flying again after some time off sitting high up in a tree that he spotted on the way back to the wagon train. He was flying high above them now, letting the air currents lift him high and bring him back down again. It felt so relaxing that he thought he would do this for a while before going back to looking at the people below. The eagle finally looked down, and he felt very good when he saw the people relaxing and working while having fun. *All is good,* he thought as he flew away.

It was very late in the afternoon when screams were heard coming from the east end of the circled wagons. Everyone was running to that end of the encampment, trying to see what was wrong or why someone was screaming so loud. Pete arrived quickly and saw a man on horseback to the southeast side of the valley near the mountain. The man was sitting on a huge bay-colored gelding with a completely white face. The horse was beautiful, and the man on his back was big and dirty looking, like a man who had been on the trail for some time.

Pete grabbed Old Jim, quickly saddled him, and started riding out to see who the man was and what he wanted. He heard some of the men behind him scurrying to find their horses and getting the saddles and other equipment on board along with their rifles or shotguns. It must have been over a mile across the meadow to the southeast before Pete could see the man's face, and it sent a chill down his spine. This man had been in a battle somewhere in his life that had almost killed him. He had a scar down the side of his face from his hairline by his left ear down the center of his jaw to his Adam's apple. It was overgrown with wide, deep scar tissue. The sun had made the skin on his face rough and pitted, which made the big scar stand out even more.

Pete pulled Old Jim to a halt in front of the stranger and said, "Howdy, what is your name, Mister?"

The man sitting on the bay just stared at Pete with one of the coldest looks ever given and, after a few minutes, said, "Alfred, that's my God-given name, but most call me Big Al." Pete suggested that he join the wagon train for the evening, if not longer, and Big Al agreed. So together, they turned the horses around and headed to the campsite.

As they turned the horses, Pete saw the Colt .45 long barrel in the man's holster, and he knew then that they had better be careful around this man. Big Al seemed like a very nice man but one who could tear you apart or kill you just as easy as he could love you. Something here seemed strange to Pete.

Everyone in camp liked to hear the stories that Big Al told as well as the accent that he had. It was different from the normal old Norski they all had heard since they were children. While Big Al was the new excitement in camp and very busy, Pete decided to look around for clues about him. He went to his horse and checked its feet, which told him the horse had not been ridden on soft ground but rather hard, rocky ground. This horse had been in the high country around this valley on the mountainsides. Then Pete looked at his saddle and gun scabbard, where he saw another 1861 Henry. He also saw an extra holster with a new-looking Colt .45 inside it. Several knives were hanging down from the saddle horn too. The saddlebags were homemade from some of the best deer hides available with fancy stitching all along the sides. Pete wondered what was inside them.

Pete was walking back into camp, now wondering where, why, and how this big man had gotten here and where he was headed and why. Was he a trapper, a scout, a mountain man, a thief, or a wanted outlaw? Or was he a lawman looking for an outlaw? He decided he had better get several men to watch camp tonight just in case something bad was going to happen. Before they turned out for the night, he was also going to ask Big Al a lot of questions and then try to figure it out.

Pete wandered to the group of people who surrounded Big Al and listened to the stories he was telling. The people were asking many of the questions that Pete wanted, so he just listened very carefully to the answers, trying to hear if they sounded truthful, rehearsed, or not relevant. Most of the answers sounded pretty truthful, but they were spoken by a man who definitely had experience in the high country that surrounded the wagon train.

Pete then asked, "How long have you lived here in the high country, and where did you come from?" He watched Big Al's face very carefully for any kind of tell, a twitch, a blinky eye, a change of volume in his voice, or a quiver in it.

Big Al sat there for a moment thinking and moving his eyes around in small circles, and finally, he spoke. "I have been in this high country, give or take a hundred miles any direction, for about thirty years now. I know it like the back of my hand. I know which plants to eat and which ones not to eat, which Indians are friends and which are not, when the snow will be here and when it will leave again, and where the best places are to hunt and which are not any good at all." Pete felt comfortable with his answer and thought he could depend on this man if he was ever in need of help.

Pete was now lying under his wagon, head on the old saddle, trying to sleep, but that was not coming on like he had hoped. He kept thinking of the questions and the answers, wondering if they were the truth or not. Then he remembered that Big Al had not told them where he came from. Was this planned or just a forgotten part of the question? He would have to remember to ask Big Al soon that very question, and it would have to be when they were face-to-face so that Pete could see his eyes.

Pete was an honest man who always insisted that he could see the truth come through a man's eyes, and he was convinced that it was the truth. He would have to put Big Al to the test in the next few days before everyone in camp started trusting him too much. Keeping people moving and staying together down a trail was hard work, but so was keeping people from becoming too trusting too quickly. Wow, *how is this going to work?* he wondered as he dozed off to sleep.

Big Al was lying awake too. He was thinking about the nice, innocent people he had befriended tonight and how that may pay dividends later. He also felt like Pete was pushing or, better yet, prying into his past somewhat, and he did not like that feeling. As he dozed off, he too thought he would have to check things out more in the next few days.

They had two men at each end of the camp tonight as watchmen overall, and they were grumbling about why they needed more men tonight. Of all the nights to beef up the security, this was the worst because they were up late already, and this would make it harder to have enough rest.

Far away high up in his tree sat the eagle. He was wide awake as well, wondering why he couldn't go to sleep. He had not checked on his friends lately and was wondering what had been happening out in the valley below. As he too dozed off to sleep, he thought that tomorrow would be a great day to check in on them.

Early the next morning, Pete was up before sunrise, walking to the east end of camp to check on the night watchmen. When he arrived, he sat down on a log and started talking with Fred Jonesburg and Lars Larson about the events of the night. They shared that everything was very normal for the night except they thought they had seen someone walking through the camp at around midnight and go into the area where the horses were tied. When they checked it out, all the horses were accounted for, and they did not see anyone either. Pete was wondering if that could have been Big Al. A mountain man would have skills where he could slip in and out before anyone would know about it. Pete thought maybe Big Al was just testing them to see what skills they had, or maybe he just needed something from his saddlebags. *Hmmm.*

Pete walked down through the camp, watching from side to side, looking to see if everything was in place. It appeared to be fine, but something told him to keep checking, and he did not like the feeling at all. He noticed that the big mountain man was rolled up in his buffalo robe as he passed by, slowly looking. When he reached the other end, he asked the boys down there if they had seen anything out of the ordinary during the night, and both of them shook their head to say no.

The eagle left his perch high up in the tree very early this morning, thinking he would get a head start on the day. First, he flew straight across the valley and halfway up the mountainside, and then he started flying eastward. There was not one sign of the Crow war party anywhere. Then it happened again, that twinkle of light way, way to the east. The eagle headed east to see what his friends were doing.

Forty minutes later, he was flying high above them, still unnoticed. He saw the smoke rising from their campfires and could smell some bacon frying and hear the voices down below. The eagle had been flying overhead for quite some time when he noticed a big man near the center of the camp talking to a group of people, so he used his keen eyesight to zero in on the man. He saw that the man was somewhat out of place down there as he did not appear clean shaven or, for that matter, clean at all—long whiskers, bear claw necklace, buffalo robe for a jacket, and mule skin boots on his feet. Then he noticed the ugly big scar on the man's cheek. *That should be an alarm for them,* he thought. The eagle was wondering if this was a friend or an enemy. *Time would tell the story.* He started to fly toward the mountainside, looking for something to eat. As he was leaving the camp, he noticed the little twinkle of light again and then again. His thoughts went to Anna as he flew south.

Anna was busy making bacon and sliced potatoes with a few eggs over the campfire. She had enough here for Pete, herself, and Big Al, if he wanted to join them. She thought it was kind of nice to have a stranger in camp with them, and it reminded her of when they had visitors in Iowa. Anna was hoping that Pete would return before Big Al came over, if he was going to do that. She wasn't sure enough of herself to start or keep a conversation going with a stranger. Soon Pete was standing there, and he asked when breakfast would be ready and if Big Al had been by their campsite. Anna said it would be ready soon and that she had not seen Big Al.

Just then, Big Al came around the corner of the wagon and said, "Good morning." Both Pete and Anna greeted him as well. The men sat down on a couple of logs that were makeshift chairs and began talking. First, it was all small talk about the weather and how hot it may get today, and then it shifted to more serious stuff.

Pete asked him where he was born, and he said without missing a beat, "Northern New York State."

Pete was sure that was the truth and passed on to the next question that bothered him. "What do you do for a living?"

Big Al sat back for a second and said, "I've done just about everything you can do to make a living, except undertaker. That is one line of work I don't want. Currently, I am not working, just doing a little trapping here and there. I used to be a scout for the cavalry, the Union side, but that ended when the war ended. I know every tribe of Indians around here. Have you had any run-ins with them?" Pete informed him of the Cheyenne and the Ute and said they didn't bother much. It seemed like they were not too worried about the wagon train or where they were going.

Big Al just sat there awhile thinking, and then he asked which trail they had taken in getting here. Pete replied that they had been on the south by southwest trail when they suddenly found themselves lost. They were suddenly in a beautiful country with very tall straight-up mountain walls of many colors and snow on the tops of the mountains with cottonwood trees all around. Also, there were many small meadows with streams running through them. Flowers were everywhere as well as deer and antelope.

Pete stopped talking because Al's face was as white as a ghost. Then he asked why Al's color had drained from his face. Big Al cleared his throat and started to talk. "Did you notice any Indians when you were going through this area?" Of course, Pete shook his head to say no. Then Big Al continued, "I noticed about ten miles west of here about eight or nine sets of horse hoofprints that were headed east at a high rate of speed. Then they stopped, turned around, and went west just about as fast as they came. It didn't make sense to me at the time, but now it does. They were Crow, and they were young braves on the warpath. One or two of them had dropped feathers that were only used while they are on the warpath. Someone or something had scared them, and they were heading to the main camp to recruit more braves, I'll bet you."

He continued, "The beautiful place you came through was the Crow burial grounds, which are the holiest places the Crow have. They will hunt all of you down until they have killed every last person who trespassed on their ancestors' holy resting spot. They are the worst of the worst when it comes to torture. They will kill you fast or very slow, depending on the day and how they feel about you. We are all in trouble now and will have to keep an eye out at all times for the Crow, no more rest until we are far enough away or dead. And neither one will be enough."

Breakfast was over, and both Big Al and Pete could only think of the Crow and where they were now. Pete then asked, "Should you and I go out into the forest on each side of the valley and look for them?"

Nobody said a word for several minutes when Big Al said, "I think we should go to the spot where I saw their hoofprints in the ground and follow them for quite some time until we determine where they are or where they are going." They both agreed and started walking to their horses to saddle up.

Chapter 4

Big Al and Pete met at the west end of the camp on horseback. Each of them led a mule alongside the horses packed with just about everything you would need on a trip of three weeks—shovels, tents, blankets, beef jerky, frying pans, and many other things that would be needed, such as rope, a few sticks of dynamite, and bullets for the big 1861 Henrys. The mules were trying to get their legs underneath themselves for this trip, so they were kind of squirming around with their feet, trying to adjust the load until Pete had had enough and yelled at them to stop it. It was amazing how fast they could stop the BS and stand still.

Pete nudged Old Jim, and they started down the meadow to the west, with Big Al beside him on his horse. Just then, Pete asked Big Al what his horse's name was, and he replied, "Ghost because of his white head." Then they rode on for several miles without saying a word.

Here, Big Al took the lead with Pete following as they crossed the stream on the north side of the valley and headed up into the mountainside. As they were going up, Big Al stated that they should keep going until they hit the trail about halfway up where the Crow had been. Then they should follow it west to where the Crow had been camped to see if they could learn anything from the campsite. They would make camp there tonight.

The eagle flew overhead to the east, where he saw the two guys riding on the north side of the mountain about halfway up on the trail with heavy packs on the mules. He was thinking that they must be going for a long ride and must intend to stay awhile too. The eagle thought, *The Crow might be coming back, and if that was true, would they meet the two men somewhere on the trail? Wow, that could get real ugly fast.* He flew east to see what was going on at the wagon train.

He saw that the people in the camp were acting as if nothing was wrong at all, and it was business like normal. Ole Olsen must have been out hunting this morning because a group of younger people were gathered in the center of the circle, taking the hide off a couple of buffalo. They were big older bulls with big horns and many battle scars on their hide. The grass was somewhat flattened out now that the camp had been here a few days. *Soon they would have paths in the grass from the wear of walking constantly,* he thought as he flew to a nearby tree.

Anna was having a happy day washing some shirts and pants for Pete and some dresses for herself along with socks for both of them. She was singing and smiling all day, and every once in a while, she wondered about Pete and Big Al. She thought they might have a lot to talk about or very little, depending on how it all started out. Anna was sure that the two men could become very good friends, if they would just accept each other without trying to "figure each other out" as Pete would sometimes say.

Big Al and Pete had reached the Crow campsite halfway up the mountainside just before dark, which allowed them time to scout around the campsite and the surrounding meadow. They were sitting around the campfire now, discussing what they had learned. Both of them agreed there were eight to ten Crow here with horses in the meadow a few days ago, and they were ready for war. Pete had found some war feathers with signs of berry paint in some leaves nearby. He asked Big Al how they made the war paint, and Big Al said it was a mix of berries, mud, and bear grease that had a horrible smell to a white man, but it didn't seem to bother the Crow.

The fire was roaring from dead oak limbs, which were very dry and burned like gasoline. They had bedrolls laid out, with saddles used as pillows and cargo used as shields from attacks. The cargo would stop most arrows and spears but not bullets. Horses were hobbled and let loose in the meadow, with Old Jim tied close by just in case something or someone scared their horses and they started running. Horses could run with hobbles on if they were scared into a full gallop instantly. At a full run, horses moved their front legs in unison but until they reached full speed, they didn't.

The guys talked about the Crow some more, and Big Al said he thought they knew about the wagon train going through the holy land of the Crow. He thought they were coming to avenge it when something scared them. He wondered what could have scared the Crow enough to leave a small wagon train that appeared as an easy target. Could it be a big spirit or something about the group?

Then Big Al thought of the big 1861 Henry and asked if Pete had fired it in the last few days. He nodded that he had when he shot the deer that was out in front of him by seven hundred feet. Then he remembered the twinkle that had caught his eye from up on this mountainside. He then told Big Al he had stared toward the mountain for a long time before he went back to work.

Big Al sat up and rubbed his chin before he said, "I think the Crow most likely sent Awanatu with some braves to kill all of you and capture your horses and supplies. They were scouting you out when you fired the big Henry, which scared them half to death. The Crow have seen the damage an 1861 Henry can do, and they don't want anything to do with it. They are brave but not so much that they will do dumb things in spite of it. I would guess they went back to the Crow main camp to get more braves and weapons. They will be back stronger than ever."

Pete nodded in agreement and then asked, "What do we do next?"

Big Al said they would need to think about it tonight and come up with a plan soon. "A mountain man could fight them better than a bunch of farmers, but it is what it is." Maybe they would need to move faster or dig in and defend themselves, and either had advantages and disadvantages. Pete asked if they should go back one day's ride to the good campsite that was slightly elevated and dig in. Both of them agreed to sleep on it and talk again in the morning.

Before they fell asleep, Al stated that the Crow would be gone for at least a week or more. They would expect the train to be farther west, so they would be coming east, careful not to miss the settlers. "This would give us extra time," he said as they fell asleep.

The Crow had arrived at Buffalo Run and were gathered around the campfire, discussing the wagon train's future. They were eating, talking about the settlers, and discussing the best place to ambush them. The chief wanted all the scalps to hang from the lodgepoles once they had inflicted torture on the palefaces. "We would discuss it more after a good night's sleep," he said as they wandered off to their own tepees.

Back at the wagon train, Anna wondered how Pete and Big Al were getting along high up in the mountains. She was sure it was going very good, but she still wondered. Everyone was sleeping except the guards at each end of the camp. *I better join them,* she thought. High up in his tree, the eagle was fast asleep, dreaming about all his friends.

Oh-y-Yee was walking around the meadow with the hobbles on, looking for good grass to eat, when the sun came up over the mountaintops. The rest of the horses were eating alongside her and enjoyed it just as much as she did. They had been here for several days now, and she was wondering why they had the big hurry back along with the sudden rest, which everyone seemed to enjoy. Oh-y-Yee was not in a hurry to leave either because she was treated like a queen now, with Awanatu coming to her several times a day, brushing her hair, and playing with her. He did not seem like himself because he was so relaxed and kind. She almost started to like him.

Awanatu was up eating a little jerky and sitting by the campfire, enjoying the heat. Most of the camp was moving around to get by the campfire to take off the chill of the night. *Nothing beats a good hot fire,* thought Awanatu. Everyone was enjoying the heat, some food, and the fresh air that was blowing toward them from the northwest. It was slightly chilly unless you were by the campfire or in the tepee under your buffalo robe.

A few braves were coming down the mountainside on their way back toward the campsite from a hunting trip. It looked like they were successful because ten or twelve horses were packed with buffalo hides filled with meat. This would make a happy tribe of Crow people, and tonight there would be a feast and dancing.

But between now and then, there would be a lot of hard work. Some of them would be cutting the meat into long strips and drying them for a few days over the fire to make jerky for later. Some would be scraping the excess fat off the hides and some drying them so that they could make them into blankets and robes; some owould be making knife handles from the horns and needles from the smaller bones. Not one piece of the buffalo would be wasted. It was a sin in the Crow nation to kill an animal and not use all of it for your needs. This was why the Crow did not like the palefaces. The Crow would love to do to the paleface just what they had done to the buffalo: shoot them, take their hair, and leave them on the ground to rot—nothing more and nothing less.

Last night's meeting was only among the top-ranking Crow warriors and chieftains. Many things were discussed, but the main reason for the meeting was the paleface people traveling east of here and the fact that they had traveled through the sacred grounds of the Crow. It was a lively meeting with many songs and dances of what each warrior would do to them when they were captured. The tribal committee decided that the Crow would rest here for several weeks while the palefaces came closer to this camp. Then they would be rested and ready for war with the weaker palefaces, who would be feeling safe. The Crow also talked about the countryside around them and said they would surprise the settlers in a midday attack when they were not close to water. The settlers' horses would be tired as well, and they would be getting thirsty too. This morning was very exciting to the Crow, for all they had to do was prepare.

The wagon train was awake and moving around next to the blazing fire to take the chill off them. Some were making breakfast and some gathering firewood and water while waiting for some food. *This is going to be a nice day,* thought Anna as she started to work.

She was also thinking of Pete and Big Al, wondering where they were and what they were talking about. "I wonder if they are friends," she thought out loud and then again was lost in more thoughts.

After breakfast, Anna saw that everyone was doing some of the common chores around the wagon train. Ole had been out hunting with some of the men, and they brought back two elk. *This would be a nice change from deer and buffalo,* she thought. Children were playing around the stream or helping with the chores, and the young men were cutting more firewood.

Her thoughts went back to Pete and Big Al, and she was still wondering if they were friends or enemies or if one of them was dead. Anna's thoughts went back to her childhood Sunday school class and remembered the song "Jesus Loves Me." This song always gave her comfort and peace, and she needed that right now. It was lonely enough out here in the deserted part of the world with Pete, and she could not imagine what it would be like without him. Then she thought about asking God to deliver him home safely, so she went to their wagon, got the old Bible from one of the drawers, and began to read. After reading the Good Book for quite some time, she prayed like she had never prayed before, almost screaming and begging God to help them make it to their new home somewhere in the west.

The horses and cattle were grazing nearby with long rye and orchard grass available and a stream of cold mountain water running down and through the valley.

Chapter 5

The Mountain Lion

Far away in the mountains, Big Al was cleaning his big knife that he called Slasher. It was covered in blood, and one could see that it was dull from cutting through bones and sinew. It had been a very long and tough battle that he thought he had lost several times. Just when he had the advantage, it seemed to slip away from him because of his bloody hands slipping from the big knife's handle or the fact that he would be stabbed in the back again. Several times, he thought he would lose his life; but each time, he rebounded to take control of the fight and finally killed the assailant.

He had not seen the big mountain lion until it jumped from the tall pine tree. The lion had just caught the front right shoulder near the joint and had missed most of the muscle and sinew, catching mostly his thick rawhide vest. Al had been hurt the most by the fall off his horse and was lucky when the lion came again right after he had gathered his knife, Slasher. The mountain lion almost ran straight into the blade, which slowed him down considerably. If the lion had not run out of blood, Big Al would have died that day. He thought now about the blood he had lost too. *Is it more than I thought?* he wondered because his back felt like it had been ripped wide open.

Now he was wondering how long it would be before Pete would find him. They had split up earlier in the day so that they could find some sign of the Crow or game because they needed to know where both of them were. Pete had taken the trail that led up into the high country, and Al had taken the lower trail, which he was sure would have signs of the Crow or maybe even the Crow themselves. Big Al knew the Crow quite well and was sure he could talk with them and find out more information. This would buy more time for the group of settlers. Now he would just have to wait until Pete showed up.

Pete was riding Jim high up in the mountains when everything went eerily silent for what seemed like three minutes but was really only a few seconds. Animals always shut down their noise and movements when there was danger around, and this was what they had done. Pete had stopped Jim, and they had listened for several minutes but heard nothing. They even listened after the birds started singing again. Now they were just checking for signs of the Crow or big game for their food. Neither sign was found, so Pete decided to head for their campsite to see if Big Al was there already.

Pete reached the campsite just to find out that nobody had been there in a long time. This sent a chill up his spine. Big Al should have made camp an hour ago because he did not have to go up to the higher trail and then back down. Did the Crow find him? Did they kill him? Were they talking, or did he have an accident? Pete decided to go east on the lower trail to try to find Al. He was sure that he would have to be careful, or he too might end up dead.

Pete let Jim have a little bit of grass and water and then rubbed him down before they saddled up. Jim was tired and slow at first but then kind of fell into a steady gait that was very comfortable for Pete. This was one of the best horses that he had ever owned; he was not that big, but he was very nimble and quick, a great horse for the mountains and rocky terrain.

The sun was getting lower in the sky now, and Pete was worried that he may not have time to find Big Al before dark. *Then what?* he thought. *Do I continue to ride, looking for him, or do I stop and make camp?* It was a good question that carried with it two different outcomes. With continuing, Big Al would get help quicker, and that was important if he was injured and bleeding. The second idea was to make camp, and that too was good if Big Al was not hurt but was only talking with the Crow. Going at night would not be good if Pete stumbled on Big Al and the Crow war party at their campsite. All hell would break lose then, and most likely, neither Al nor Pete would survive.

Big Al was lying on a patch of thick grass just off the trail near the tall pine tree, which the mountain lion had jumped from earlier today. He had taken the skinned hide off the lion and was using it to keep warm. He had also drunk some of the blood to help him stay awake and alert. Al was getting very sore and stiff too. He was struggling to stay awake when he fell asleep.

Far away in another big old pine tree sat the eagle. He was far away from home with a young female eagle that had flown into his territory. The old eagle went to chase her away when she started to flirt with him, and to him, that was exciting. He had forgotten all about his friends down below for many days, and now he thought of them once again. Tomorrow he would take his new friend along with him and check out the people down below just to see if anything had changed.

Pete decided it was too dangerous to continue tonight, so a few miles back, he had started looking for a good place to make camp. Tonight would be poor grass for Jim and beef jerky for Pete, and hopefully, they would have some water close by. It wasn't long before a nice spot appeared before them, a small clearing with some low bushes on one side, which he could crawl under to sleep. He would be hidden in case anyone came down the trail during the night.

Morning came after what seemed like an eternity for Big Al. He had tossed and turned all night long, trying to find a comfortable position or a softer spot to lie on or in. The bleeding had stopped now, and Al thought it was stopped by the lion's hide that was wrapped around him tightly. He was tired and was wondering if Pete was looking for him. Suddenly, Al started to tremble at the thought that had just went through his whole body and soul about Pete. What if the Crow or an animal attack had gotten him? Now Al would face a horrible death of starvation or maybe worse with another animal attack. He knew that animals could sense when their prey was weak, and they would not have a problem knowing that he was weak.

Pete had been on the trail for well over an hour when Al woke up. He had made up for a lot of time by moving much faster today than yesterday partly because he felt fresh and awake, and he had a purpose with the hurried-up attitude. It was to get to Big Al before something bad may happen or to help if something had already happened.

Just then, a small movement caught Pete's eye. It came from the little clearing ahead by the big, tall pine tree. It looked like a mountain lion was lying on the ground, waiting for the right time to ambush someone or something. He climbed down from Jim and pulled his big buffalo gun, the 1861 Henry, from the saddle scabbard. Pete was very careful to slowly lower himself to the ground and raised the Henry so he was looking down the sights toward the lion. Then he noticed blood on the side of the lion and then more blood. Just then, Big Al sat straight up and screamed in pain. Pete jumped up and yelled to the top of his lungs, "Al! Al!" again and again. "Al!"

Jim was running as fast as he could across the clearing toward Al. Big Al had heard the screams but was too weak to respond as he fell asleep again. Pete had arrived now and was wondering what to do first, second, and so on. He was surely hoping and praying that Al would survive.

Now Pete had several things to do at the same time. He had to watch for Indians, hobble the horses so they could eat some grass, and make some food for himself and some kind of broth for Big Al. This meant he would need fresh meat and needed to gather firewood and some herbs to make a fine tealike broth that had boiled animal fat in it so protein could go directly into the bloodstream rapidly. Then he thought, *Maybe I should check Al first to see how badly he really was hurt.*

Al seemed to be dehydrated and pale from the loss of blood. His breathing was somewhat labored and sounded like someone with a lung injury. Pete removed Al's shirt and saw the horror that must have lasted for at least a few minutes to say the least. Deep cuts went through the skin and flesh until they hit the ribs, and lucky for Al, they did not go through any of the ribs. He gently turned him over and found deep holes in Al's back from the big cat's canine teeth. The mountain lion had been trying to finish him off with a swift bite through the backbone. How the lion had failed was unbelievable. *Big Al must have had his big buffalo robe on with the rawhide vest underneath it for him to be this lucky,* thought Pete.

"Wow, he must have had his knife very sharp at the onset of the battle to survive," said Pete out loud.

Al must have fought the battle of his life and won. Pete would wash out the wounds the best he could for now with some boiling water from a campfire that would need to be started right now. He hurried away to grab some dry branches that would start easily and a bunch of larger ones for later too. This would have to be a large fire for several reasons—one to keep warm, one for cooking, one for boiling water for the cleaning of Al's wounds, and one to scare away any other wild animals. They would be drawn to the area by the smell of blood, but Pete knew they were always afraid of fire. Pete was tired, but he didn't even notice with all the work he needed to do.

It was morning, and the old eagle was wide awake, wondering when his new sweetheart would awaken. He thought that today would be a great day to explore the surrounding areas for all his friends down below to find out what was happening.

Pete had a roaring fire going now and had Big Al resting under and on top of a bunch of buffalo robes. This would help prevent him from going into shock. The bleeding was stopped, but Al needed his wounds cleaned and food in his belly soon.

Just then, Pete noticed a movement off to the left, just down the hill slightly. He slowly reached for the big 1861 Henry, grabbed it, and slowly pulled it out of the scabbard. He turned, and there directly in front of him was a huge buck deer. Almost with the same movement, Pete fired a shot from the big 1861 Henry, which dropped the large buck instantly. *One more detail finished,* he thought as he ran down to the buck and started to skin him out and gather the badly needed meat. *This is starting to work out pretty smoothly for us.*

Anna was wondering more about the two men this morning. She was thinking and praying that everything was going to be fine, and that she believed with all her heart.

It was going to be midday pretty soon, and Big Al needed food. Pete had put the first meat into the boiling pot, and it was starting to smell very good. It soon reminded him that he hadn't eaten for a long time either. His stomach was growling, and he was thinking about Al and wondering how long it had been since he had eaten. Soon he would be feeding Big Al like a little baby. *Just one spoon at a time,* he thought. How slow that would be.

Big Al was now groaning and moving like he was hurting very badly and was stiff and sore. Pete tried to set him up against the tree. *But that is like trying to carry your horse,* he thought. Food first and then clean the wounds was the order that Pete wanted. Now he just needed to do it.

Big Al had been fed, his wounds cleaned, and molten deer fat applied to the deep cuts. He had been awake for a minute during the ordeal but had fallen asleep before it was finished. The deer fat would keep the wounds from drying out and becoming chapped; plus, it would keep the dirt out. It looked good for the two men now.

Chapter 6

The eagle and his young female friend were flying westward now toward the Crow camp far to the west of Big Al and Pete. Just as before, he was enjoying the different air currents that would allow them to fly for hours at a time without hardly using any energy, sometimes floating upward and sometimes downward; nonetheless, it was kind of fun.

Anna and the people with the wagon train were becoming happy with the spot Pete had chosen for their campsite. There were many deer, elk, and buffalo nearby, with water running past the camp. Perfect. No one had seen any sign of Indians or other dangers, so all seemed good. Some of the men had started bringing in logs to make a small fortress at each end of the campsite to protect them more from the Indians in case they stayed longer than planned. Anna was starting to doubt her faith because she was sure that Pete would have been back some time ago along with Big Al. She grabbed her necklace and started to pray again silently.

Oh-y-Yee was starting to get bored with the easy life of grazing or lying around all day. Awanatu was paying attention to her every day by grooming her long mane and tail and riding her in their war games, pretending to conquer all who stood in his way. She enjoyed that part because she too thought she could conquer all who came before her. Oh-y-Yee was thinking that, one of the days ahead, they would be racing back to the east, and she was going to be in shape when that happened.

The warriors were becoming restless as the days came and went, and no one moved. They were young and strong and wanted to destroy the palefaces quickly.

Pete was glad this first day was over without more problems than what he had expected. Al was resting and seemed at peace. The horses were in the meadow, hobbled and eating. Pete caught Al's horse quickly because they had known each other before today. He figured they would be down here for a couple of weeks, hoping that Al could be well enough to travel back to the campsite with the wagon train then.

Pete was thinking about all the things around him as he leaned back on the trunk of the tall pine tree. He was thinking about Anna, the wagon train, if they had enough food, or if the Crow had circled around Al with an attack on the campsite. He sure hoped the people of the wagon train were safe, most of all Anna. Then he too fell asleep.

The eagle and his friend were now flying over the Crow campsite, enjoying the scene below. He was wondering why the Crow were still here in camp and the horses grazing nearby. The eagle saw Oh-y-Yee and thought that she had gained a couple of hundred pounds along with the rest of the horses. He saw the warriors and thought they had also gained weight. Everyone down below looked relaxed and seemed to enjoy the time with their friends and families, except a few of the warriors who appeared restless. With that, the eagles turned in flight toward the east to check in on the wagon train.

When the two eagles arrived the next morning over the covered wagon train, they could feel the warm air coming up to them from all the campfires. That warm air felt real nice in the damp, brisk temperatures of the morning. The morning air lifted them and lowered them without any effort on their part. The old eagle started to look down below and was surprised to see all the activities that had been going on between visits.

Paths were worn into the ground from the campsite in different directions—one from the campsite to the stream, another into the forest on the other side of the valley, and more up and down the valley from east to west. There was a new stockade at each end of the wagon train's circle too. It looked like someone started to build a fortress but had not yet finished. The old eagle mused that he had better pay more attention to everything around him more often than he had been when he thought of his lovely little female friend. She was not far away, rising in the upward currents just like he was doing before he was sidetracked. He flew closer to her, and she sort of flirted with him, and he forgot all about the people below for quite some time.

The old eagle was suddenly startled by a loud noise from below. When he looked down, he started laughing because Ole's cow had kicked the milk bucket over, and Ole was cussing like a trooper. He felt better after that because he realized that even humans had bad days. It wasn't long before the old eagle remembered Pete, Big Al, and Old Jim and did not see them below. He looked again, again, and again and then flew around, wondering where they were. He made larger and larger circles every time he went around the circle. Then he decided to keep searching until he found them.

A long ways away from the wagon train were the motionless bodies of Pete and Big Al. They were both tired and dirty. *But who cares?* thought Pete as he was dreaming away all thoughts of the day. Both of them could snore like a train going up a steep incline, and sometimes they would wake each other up at the same time. Then they would laugh and fall back to sleep quickly. Big Al was feeling better now and getting stronger by the day, even if it was only day 2 since the attack. Al was sure he would make it now that Pete had fed him and doctored his wounds. He was thankful that Pete had hurried to him soon after the accident. It was late afternoon before they woke up from their naps, and they were talking nonstop now.

They were talking about how the mountain lion had ambushed Big Al when he was looking back down the trail and how the force of the lunge had blasted him from the saddle instantly. Al said that, on his way to the ground, he was pulling his knife out and was hoping to use it. He landed so hard that he dropped it, but it bounced right back up into his hand, blade pointing directly at the lion. Just then, the lion leaped toward Al and had the blade buried deep into his chest. Pete told Al that he was the luckiest man on earth.

Both of them were chewing on some fresh jerky that Pete was trying to cure. They had a pot of animal fat boiling over the campfire so they could drink some of the powerful juices of it and use some for Al's wounds. "It is working just like the Crow said it would," commented Al. They continued talking and telling stories about this and that and the other thing for what seemed like hours.

Then Pete became serious, looked at Al, and said, "Tomorrow I will have to leave you for a while to go get more water." He waited for a reaction, but nothing came from Al. Finally, Al said it would work, but it did make him feel uneasy mainly because he couldn't defend himself from anyone or anything because of his weakened condition. Pete assured him that he would hurry and that, before he left, he would build a big campfire. That seemed to help Al feel better.

The eagles were flying around in bigger circles all the time, with no sign of Pete and Al. The old eagle was wondering if they were okay or not and was hoping they were. He and his pal would continue until they found them, whenever that might be. *Time would tell the whole story,* he thought.

As the two eagles were flying in big circles, the old male saw smoke coming up from the forest on the north side of the valley. He flew in front of his mate so that she would follow him, and together, they headed west toward the smoke. Now the old eagle felt some raindrops. He wondered how this could change things even more with the two men and the wagon train.

The next morning, Pete was awakened by a light rain hitting him in the face. He got dressed and went looking around to see how much water had arrived overnight. The campfire was roaring now, and Pete had built a small shelter from pine branches and limbs. He had to build it over Big Al because he was next to the big tree, which Pete needed for support. He thought his little shelter was pretty nice. It was warm inside, and Al said it was a big improvement from the cold, hard ground. Now both men had a bunch of pine branches to lie on and a roof overhead to keep out the rain. Sweet.

Pete started to think about this storm and wondered how long they would have before the snow started to fall for good. Then he thought about Big Al and noticed he was awake, so he asked him. He said they would be lucky if they had four to five more weeks without snow. Pete was hoping the wagon train was cutting wood and preparing for winter just in case the two did not make it back in time to move on.

Pete was now saddled up on Jim, and they were headed down the mountainside to get water. He had made some big leather deer hide containers that should hold five gallons of water each, which he was going to fill. *Bringing them back to camp could be fun,* he thought, going up the mountainside with three big bags full of water. Jim would have to work hard today.

Chapter 7

Oh-y-Yee was grazing in the pasture with the other horses, and the good grass was nearly gone, with only some slow-growing fall grasses coming on slowly. She was overweight but was very attractive with a shapely form. She was also one of the largest females the Crow had ever had, and they told stories about her every chance they had. Her color alone was amazing, but add her size and shape, and she was stunning.

Awanatu thought Oh-y-Yee was the best warhorse ever made because of her speed, size, and athletic abilities. He was going to start working her harder again toward spring so when the pale-faced settlers arrived, she would be in top shape. He had brushed her almost every day since they had arrived back at the Crow encampment. She had a long black tail and mane with the nice dark, dapple-gray color throughout, which just highlighted her in every way possible. Oh-y-Yee was the queen of the herd, and she pranced around the corral and meadows just like she knew it. All the other mares and most of the stallions stayed out of her way because they sensed her ability. Now it started to drizzle here, and she thought it was close to winter again.

The wagon train group was also feeling the rain and wondering when it would change from rain to winter snowstorms. Ole and some of the men were excited this morning because of the rain and the fact that Pete and Big Al had not returned. They were discussing a plan of what needed to be done first, second, and so on down the line. After a couple of hours, they came up with a plan.

They would start gathering more firewood by cutting down big trees and having the ox teams pull them from the forest to the outer circle of the wagon train. Then they could use them as protection now and also cut firewood from them all winter long, saving time now and also having something to do in the winter. They would work in teams to drag as many trees as they could around the train as fast as possible. Some of the trees would make a lane to the stream too, so they were protected when they went for water. *Great plan,* thought Ole.

The people of the wagon train were very busy now after a couple of days of dragging trees into place around the campsite. Ole was very happy with the progress and couldn't believe the number of trees that had been felled in just a few days. He was thinking that they should also cut down some big oak trees and trim them into upright posts for a fortress wall just in case Pete and Big Al didn't return in time to move on before winter arrived. Ole looked at all the trees lying around the circle of wagons and thought that it was a barrier in itself. *It is all about barriers,* he thought and then decided that they should have another wall. This would give them extra protection in case of a cold winter or an attack from the Crow Indians.

Ole started barking out the orders to the men about digging postholes, bringing in the oak trees, dragging them to the campsite, and then trimming them. He was going to build this first class, so he ordered another group of men to start dragging big rocks from the stream so they could lay a foundation for a central building that could serve as a kitchen and storage shed for the food they were gathering now. *This could be great,* he thought as he marked the spot where he thought the building should stand.

Anna was seeing all the building and preparing going on all around them, and she wondered if Pete was going to come back. It was starting to look like something bad had happened to them on the trail. She reached up and grabbed her locket and said a prayer.

Pete had arrived back at the camp with the water bags full and was hoisting them into a tree when Big Al hollered at him and said, "What are we going to do, drink ice cubes? You have worked hard to put the water up in the tree, but if it freezes tonight, we will have ice and not water." Pete lowered the waterskins closer to the ground and decided to put pine boughs over them to keep out the cold. He was sure it wasn't going to get below zero tonight and that they would have water in the morning.

Big Al said he was hungry and wanted to know how long it would be before they could have something besides beef jerky or boiled fat. Pete threw some jerky toward Al, laughed, and told him to dream on.

Pete sat down next to Al and asked him, "How are you doing?" Big Al said that he thought that he would be able to ride in a week or so if nothing else went wrong. Then Pete responded that he thought Al should lie low until he was very well healed, even if it was close to winter. They could always catch the wagon train or find them. By leaving now, they would get back to the train earlier than later, but it would not be worth it if Al caught an ugly infection in his wounds while on the trail.

Al complained that he was getting bored and tired of lying around like a newborn baby and that they needed to go back at the wagon train. *He could complain all he wants,* thought Pete. *But he couldn't leave here without help anyway, so why argue?*

Back at the wagon train, everything was moving in high gear, it appeared. The big tree barrier was thick and nearly impossible to get through, just as Ole had planned. The new walls, made of logs at each end of the wagon circle, was very impressive, just to say the least.

The new "town hall" at the center of the circle was used for Sunday worship, special meetings, as a mess hall, and as a storehouse for their meat and jerky. Ole was very proud of all their success and also his plan for the new "root cellar" at one end of the building. The ladies had been gathering berries and nuts from the forest around them and had all the bounty stored in the root cellar just in case they had to spend the winter here. They had also constructed a large stone and wooden fence on both sides of the trail from the circle down to the water's edge. Ole thought this would help protect them from the Indians in case of a surprise attack or at least prevent them from keeping the settlers inside the circle until they died of thirst.

He thought this whole plan was coming together just fine, and maybe they would name his little town Centerville. They were still dragging trees into and around the circle, and soon they would stop with that part of the building project and start another. *No rest for the wicked,* thought Ole as he remembered the pastor's message from last Sunday. *Maybe a church would be good soon.*

Anna was in her wagon with the covers pulled over both ends while she wept and prayed again and again. She couldn't help it after losing her son and now wondering if Pete would return. The wondering was what got her the most. She was wondering if Big Al had killed Pete or if the Indians had gotten both of them. Was there an accident that had both men hurt badly, or were they out there somewhere dying? It did not stop going through her head, so she decided to go where she always went when she was afraid, her prayer time. Anna called it by its right name too. She called it her time to talk with God directly and to make her requests known to him. It always made her feel better, and she also knew that if it was good for her, God would provide. The only thing that bothered her was the fact that her son was taken from her when he was so young. *I would find the answer someday,* she thought.

Chapter 8

The grass was waving as the wind was blowing through it, making it look almost like a sea of grass—beautiful dark green, so dark that it looked blue, with very pretty yellow daisies sticking up through the grass. The daisies were so thick that, at certain times, it covered the green-blue color of the grass. Hie temperature was near eighty-live degrees with a strong wind from the northwest that made it feel like sixty-five degrees. But it was nice to be outdoors, listening to the wind blowing through the grass, the birds singing, and all of nature's wonderful sounds.

Oh-y-Yee loved this time of the year. She didn't think it was summer or fall but the perfect time, not hot and not cold. All the horses from the Crow tribe were out here in this big pasture on the High Plains running and jumping and rolling in the tall grass. They had plenty to eat all summer, so they were somewhat overweight, which made them even better looking than before. And they were beautiful before.

Oh-y-Yee was the queen of the herd, and all the mares understood that too. *Soon,* she thought, *Awanatu would find out just how much stronger I had gotten over this summer.* It had been a great summer without many demanding trips here and there. Oh-y-Yee had reached maturity during the season, and she observed a difference in her body and mind. Now she noticed the young stallions when they pranced by with their manes and tails flying in the wind, which never happened before this summer. It was different now.

The Crow braves were restless and wanted something to do other than daily chores and hunting. Raids on settlers and other Indians, which were their enemies, would be welcomed now. The older men could feel this uneasy feeling when they were with the young warriors. The old men were wise and tried to prevent the braves from going on an unneeded warpath, and so far, they were successful. But they knew it wouldn't be long before something would set it off. After all, they reasoned that drying meat, curing buffalo hides, and making war clubs and new arrows weren't exactly exciting. The old men decided to try to get the young men involved in war games on horseback and other similar things to keep them from going on the warpath. *This would have to start soon, or war would find us before winter set in,* they thought.

All the young braves were sitting around the campfire when the elders arrived and sat down with them. Awanatu and his young braves were wondering why they came. He thought that this was odd because they always made the young men come to them. Then old Ten Bears began to talk in a soft tone like he was telling a secret. He suggested that they start working their horses more and more each day so that they were back in shape soon. Then they would be ready for the palefaces, who should be coming soon.

All the young men were happy when Ten Bears suggested that they divide up into four teams of young men to play horse polo. Each team would play three games, and the winners would then play three more to determine the champion, who would have bragging rights for the next year. The braves were very happy, and they started planning with renewed excitement.

With all the excitement in the air, they decided to have a feast with roasted buffalo and dancing. The old men went with Ten Bears to sit by the fire and enjoy smoking some old tobacco while watching the excited young braves, knowing there would be peace in the near future. The young braves and their female companions were enjoying the new sense of enjoyment brought on by the party and the war games of tomorrow.

Oh-y-Yee could hear the excitement, see the dancing, and smell the roasted meat while wondering what had changed to bring on this level of happiness. She saw Awanatu yelling and dancing as never before. The others were doing the same. Oh-y-Yee was hoping that they were not going back on the warpath. The warpath omeant long days with hard and fast trips. It would be very hard after so much time off.

Tonight, for the first time, a big strong stallion named Death Knife noticed Strong Mountain. She loved her English name more than her given name, but no one used the English name except the other horses. Death

Knife was solid black with a blaze and one rear sock that was white. He was the fastest horse in the Indian camp, even a hair faster than Oh-y-Yee. That made her try more and more, harder and harder; and sooner than later, she was going to show him.

Oh-y-Yee was dreaming now about Death Knife, and in her dream, she was thinking that they had united and shared a colt. She could only wonder if this would happen; and if it did, what color would the colt be? Dapple-gray with a blaze or other combos? *I would have to pursue him,* she thought. Tomorrow would be another day.

The next morning, the Crow campsite was moving very slowly, if at all. Hie party the night before had all of them tired out, and they were sleeping late this morning. Hie fires in the camp were almost out by now, so the old men were gathering firewood and were throwing it onto the fires. Soon the campsite had a raging fire with the sound of crackling wood in the air.

Oh-y-Yee and all the other horses were up and about, eating grass in the small meadow near the campsite. They could all hear and smell the burning wood on this cool morning. She thought it was fun to watch on the other horses running around the meadow when it was as full of dew as it was today. It left trails in the grass just like it did in the snow in the wintertime.

Oh-y-Yee was wondering where Death Knife was because she had not seen him this morning. Lately, that had been the first thing she did every morning. She thought something about him was interesting, but she didn't know what it was. She even wondered what made him look better to her than the other stallions but couldn't figure out what that was. Some of the horses had eaten their fill of grass now, and they were starting to lie down here and there to rest while digesting the wet grass.

Her muscles were very stiff and sore from all the running yesterday during the polo war games, in which Awanatu and she had won. Oh-y-Yee was very proud of the fact that she was the fastest and strongest horse on the field. She had several chances to oust him from her back, but she had decided that, somewhere down the road, there would be a better place to do it—somewhere out in the High Desert when no one else was around to help Awanatu or, better yet, when they were on the warpath. Going against another group of settlers or Indians would offer the perfect time for an ouster. Planning would now take place.

Awanatu was just getting into the swing of things when he started thinking about yesterday. He thought of the pride he had in his horse, for she was the best one the Crow had or had ever had. Not only was she fast and strong but she also was extremely good looking. Wow, *I am lucky to have captured her when she was young,* he thought. Oh-y-Yee would have been uncontrollable if he found her a year later. Awanatu also loved the fact that they were the best group of warriors in the whole Crow nation. That made him the number three man in the tribe.

The old men and women were also happy to see the renewed attitude throughout the tribe. The enactment of the battle was good for everyone. The children were all excited about the war games too. Sitting idly was boring unless you had been working hard for a long time.

Speaking of being idle, the old eagle was out hunting for food with his mate when he happened to see smoke rising far, far away down the valley. *Someday soon,* he thought, *I and my friend would have to fly around the territory to see what is happening everywhere.* He had the settlers, Pete and Big Al, and all the Crow to check in on.

It was getting colder at night now, so they had been more content to just sit around in their tree nest talking and cleaning the lice out of each others feathers. *What a life,* he thought as he spied something running along close to the ground. With his great eyesight, he realized it was a pocket gopher who was searching for his hole. The old eagle hurried as fast as he could and swooped down with one of his talons extended and grabbed the little fellow. It was just enough for him, but he shared it with his princess. Then they would search for another lost soul, and again, they were off flying around.

The fires were burning brightly at the campsite of the settlers too. They were all up and had gathered at the central building for breakfast. They had some wild turnips, some beef jerky, berries, and other wild fruits of the prairie along with some fresh-baked bread. Ole had been up early and had milked his old cow and now was churning the butter. They were going to have a Thanksgiving feast today. It was a tradition in Norway that they would have a feast when all the crops had been harvested for the year. Hie root cellar was full of wild turnips, potatoes, berries and other fruits, jams, dried beef jerky, canned meat, wild honey, and every kind of nut imaginable. *We have a lot to be thankful for,* thought Ole.

Anna was in her wagon having her morning talk with the Lord. She was trying to have faith that Pete would be okay, but three months was a long time to wonder if he was going to come home again. She did something different today because she not only asked God to help but also demanded help from him because he was her Father. Anna thought that if God was her Father, he should know how she felt. She ended her prayer as always by saying, "If it is your will, please let it be done."

It was a beautiful day with many smells in the air—the smoke from the campfires, the smell of cooking food, and the smell of God's great creation. How lucky could a person be!

Hie morning air was kind of humid high up on the mountainside where Big Al was lying in his bed made out of pine branches and bows. He could smell the coffee brewing on the campfire down below him. It was about twenty-five feet away from him, but it could just as well have been a mile. Al was not recovering very fast, nor was all this lying around helping him move any quicker. He was thinking that the mountain lion must have pinched a nerve near his spine when the attack occurred that affected his lower back and legs. The legs would not hold him up when he tried to stand, and they were slow to react when he tried moving quickly.

Big Al was not a complaining type of guy but would rather keep it on the inside away from others. But it worried him. He did not have anyone to depend on, and he didn't want to start now with that kind of bullshit. Al had always looked down on someone who couldn't take care of themselves. Now he was going to face that himself.

Al was sure that Pete was out and about, looking for small game like pheasants, doves, or quail. He was just thankful that Pete had been taking such good care of him. Not only had he done a great job but he also had become a very good friend. that wasn't always an easy thing with Big Al, for he had many years alone out in this vast forest that made him set in his ways. Al was hoping Pete would hurry up because he felt like he was going to starve to death soon.

Big Al was thinking that today he should talk Pete into leaving this camp and heading back to the wagon train even if he wasn't completely well or healed 100 percent. Winter was just around the corner.

Pete was about three to four miles from camp, looking for small prairie chickens, when he noticed that all the birds stopped singing at the same time. He froze in his tracks. All his senses were on high alert now while standing motionless; his eyes searched to the right slowly and then back to the left. While going back and forth, they also went up and down, searching again as they moved. Pete found nothing, but his senses were telling him that something was wrong when the birds suddenly stopped singing. He was glad he was holding his old 1861 Henry in the ready position while frozen in time.

Slowly, he reached around the stock and released the safety. He was slowly looking right to left when he felt like someone was looking at him from above. He pulled the hammer back and jerked the rifle upward at the same time as his eyes looked upward, and he saw a big cat jumping down toward him. During the next two seconds, everything seemed to happen at once—big cat coming down, rifle going up, Pete landing on his backside, and the big 1861 Henry bellowing like a cannon twice.

Pete woke up lying in a pool of blood, which was warm and sticky. He couldn't move. He looked around the best he could, but this heavyweight was on his back, holding him down. Pete wiggled, squirmed, pushed, and kept doing it harder and harder until the weight moved to the side. Then and only then was he relieved in what he saw—the big mountain lion was lying there dead. *The big cat must have weighed close to four hundred pounds,* thought Pete. Wow!

He was very tried, but he stood up and brushed the dirt from his shirt and pants. He started shaking uncontrollably. Wow, he thought, *the same mountain lion that had jumped Big Al.* After a few minutes, he stopped shaking and regained control of himself when he thought of Big Al and how worried he must be. *Better hurry up and get some prairie chickens.* Now he was very hungry too.

Pete arrived back in camp about three hours later than he planned. He brought with him the skinned mountain lion and head along with some prairie chickens that they could cook quickly. Needless to say, Big Al was pissed and hungry, and he chewed out Pete up one side and down the other. When he was finished, Pete said, "Well, I am glad to see you missed me."

Things settled down pretty good then, and Pete told Al about the whole morning's excitement. Al was shocked about the mountain lion and wondered out loud if that old son of a bitch had jumped other people along the trail, maybe for many years. "Once ambushing humans gets into a lion's mind, it is all they can think about—ambush, ambush."

The day was warming up somewhat, but it looked like it might start raining later in the day. Big Al was happy now that his stomach was full and that Pete was safe. He thought it was a good time to talk about moving back toward the wagon train, so he started the conversation. Pete listened for what seemed like hours as Big Al tried to convince him that he was fine and could travel. When Al had finished, Pete looked him square in the eyes and told him that the trip would be very hard and that it would take five or six days to complete, but it needed to be done and soon. He continued on about the weather changing and winter rolling in any day now, so it would be better to be with the train than holed up here all winter. He continued on by saying that maybe he could cut some long poles and cross them up over Big Al's horse and then make a bed behind the horse for Al to rest on. The idea sounded good to both of them. Pete said, "First, we had better kill a deer and make some beef jerky before we start because time would be short on the trail." Big Al agreed.

Now the people of the wagon train had almost given up on Pete and Big Al. Some of them were saying that Big Al must have killed Pete for the big 1861 Henry and Old Jim, and others thought the Crow had lifted their scalp. Most of these thoughts came out after they had seen Anna crying or sitting off to the side by herself.

No matter what the story was, they all thought they knew the correct outcome of Pete and Al. They knew little about themselves, the Crow, the winter ahead, or Pete and Al. They were about to learn a lot about surviving the long cold winter of the northern Plains.

This afternoon, the wind had shifted from the south to a stronger wind coming from the northwest, which had dropped the temperature over twenty degrees in about a half-hour. All the wild animals had noticed this slight change in the air temperature and humidity levels. To them, the days were even slightly shorter now than before. They were all in a hurry to gather food or eat more to gain weight before the snow and ice came in like a roaring lion.

Pete felt the change in the air, but he did not say anything to Big Al mainly because he did not want to make Al get in a hurry and try to do too much with his sore, aching body. He was thinking that they had better hurry up and get a move on things before they were trapped by deep snow and cold weather. Big Al would not survive that kind of change. Pete decided to find two tall pines to cut for lodgepoles that would go on each side of Al's horse and also to find small branches for the bed today and not tomorrow. So off he went into the forest, careful not to get ambushed by another wild cougar or mountain lion.

Big Al was lying on his bed, carving crutches, and trying to weave grapevines into the pine branches making his bed. It was slow work and sometimes hard to do. He too was thinking they had better hurry up and get back to the train soon. Many years when he was up in these mountains trapping, he would see the winds change suddenly, and then a huge storm would appear out of nowhere. Often it would dump several feet of snow overnight, and then the strong northwest wind would start blowing, and it would get extremely cold fast. *No human will survive it. That is a fact,* thought Al.

Pete had two long pine poles tied to Old Jim as he walked alongside him. He noticed that Old Jim's hair was getting thick and quite long, which was another sign that winter was due in soon. Pete had a sense of urgency in his step now compared with a week ago. *Tomorrow morning, we will start out very early toward the wagon train, and Anna,* he thought. Then his mind started to play with him with thoughts like *What if the Crow had come back and wiped them out or some sickness had found the train?* His heart was racing faster and faster until he could hardly stand it. Pete stopped just as quickly as he had started and, in one motion, dropped to his knees and asked God to help him reach the train safely and to also find the people there safe too. Afterward, he felt a lot better.

Ole had noticed the big change of the winds also and was wondering if Pete and Big Al were still alive or if they had been done in. Ole reflected for a minute and then thought it would have taken the whole Crow nation to wipe them out. They were naturals in the mountains and had a big advantage with their big 1861 Henrys. *They are coming back soon* was his last thought on the subject, and he hurried off because he too had work to do.

The old eagle and his princess had also noticed the change in the air as they sat in the big nest high up in the big pine tree. Snow would be flying soon.

The Crow had been playing their war games polo each day now for some time, and both the horses and their riders were showing huge improvements in their skills. They also could tell that winter was coming, and they were prepared with all kinds of nuts and grains stored up along with the normal amounts of buffalo jerky. They had a pile of wood next to their lodges as well.

It was getting later in the evening when the wind picked up suddenly. The wind started blowing hard out of the northwest, bringing the temperatures down very fast and blowing dried leaves and dust ahead of its sudden bursts. If you were outside in the path of the wind, it was hard to see anything at all; plus, it was very cold. The wild animals were looking for a safe place to hide behind a fallen tree or a cave or sometimes just behind a knoll on top of a hill. Anything that you could use to shield yourself from that nasty wind was good.

The Crow were inside their tepees with a roaring fire going in each of them. They were too warm. They could now hear some light rain hitting the sides of their tepees, and it was soothing to hear. The old Indian men said that it was the Great Spirit talking to everyone and telling them that they too should be thankful for what they had.

Oh-y-Yee and the rest of the herd were lying in the meadow just over a crest of the hill that was closest to the camp. It was pretty comfortable until this rain started coming down hard. It had a way of stinging, so all the horses turned so that their backside was toward the rain. They would form a tight group with all their behinds facing the same direction and their heads down, looking forward to predators. Their eyes were looking forward, and their nostrils were smelling the wind, which was coming from behind them. This way, no one could or would surprise them with an attack.

The old eagle and his friend were perched in an old tree that had thick branches all around and above to protect them from the rain.

The settlers were all in their wagons, listening to the wind blow and the rain hit the sides of the carriages. They were worried about the wind ripping the covers off the wagons, leaving everything and everyone exposed to the elements. Ole was thinking about Pete and Big Al and was wondering how they were doing or if they were doing at all. He also thought that the camp's hunters had better keep hunting for deer, antelope, and buffalo while the weather was changing, and the women could make it into jerky. They were going to spend the winter right here, and if that was to be successful, they needed to get more trees downed and put around the east end of their small town. *Always more work too.*

Pete and Big Al were having a very rough evening. *The night is going to be worse,* thought Pete. The wind was blowing hard up on their side of the mountain, and with it came rain. It was running down the mountainside, making the ravines impassable for a few days, just when they needed to go. The going would be much slower now with rain falling and making dust into mud everywhere. The horses would slow down, making sure of every foothold before placing weight on it; plus, the bed/sled for Al would pull harder and slower.

Tomorrow would have to take care of the things of itself, thought Pete as he dozed off to sleep.

The next morning was bright and beautiful, with the sun shining brightly around the forest, putting a bright green color to the trees. The color was amazing, but the smell in the air was even better; the smell was clean and fresh like never before. The birds were singing as they flew from tree to tree, looking for something to eat. They were also cleaning themselves in the little pools of fresh new water. Pete was awake, chewing on some jerky, when Al awakened. *Today is going to be the biggest test well ever have,* thought Pete. What he didn't know was that Al was thinking almost the same thing.

Over an hour later, Pete had Old Jim saddled and ready as well as Big Al's horse. Now he was wondering how he would get Al from his hammock to the pole sled behind his horse. Just as he was wondering about that, Big Al was standing by his tree, bellowing out orders about bringing his horse by so he could flop into the pole bed as he called it. And that was just what he did. They started off down the trail, with Pete looking ahead, making sure that the pathway was wide enough for the whole pole bed. *It is going to be real tricky,* he thought when they started going down the steep part of the mountain. He could hardly wait.

Today the wind had died down, but it was still rather cold outside. Pete was warm from walking and working, but he had to keep his eyes on Big Al, who was just lying there close to the cold ground. They were traveling now on an old game trail that Al thought had been used for several hundred years because the paths were worn even through the stone and big rocks. The going was good, and they were making good time.

Big Al was in pain every time the pole or poles would hit a high spot or rock on the trail. That sudden jar felt like it went through his entire body like an electric jolt. It hurt more on the inside than the outside, and Al was wondering if he could make it to the settlers' campsite without passing out completely.

Now they were traveling across a meadow, and that was soothing in more than one way for Big Al. It was smooth, so the ride was good, and the meadow had a good growth of grass that blocked out the strong northwest wind. It was blowing hard, and it was cold, very cold. Al was moving his fingers constantly, trying to keep them warm, but it wasn't working very well. He would have to hang on with one hand at a time while the other hand was under the buffalo robe that covered most of his body. It was a good thing that he was very strong from all his hunting and trapping trips up and down these mountain slopes. He had been in excellent shape before the attack by the mountain lion, and that was why he was still alive, he was sure.

Pete halted up ahead slightly and was looking all around as if something was wrong. Big Al's horse continued to move forward until he was abreast of Pete's horse, Old Jim. Al spoke very softly when he said, "What are we stopping for?" There was no response, so Al knew that something was different ahead, so he kept his mouth shut for the time being.

Pete slid out of his saddle like a big cat on the prowl, softly hitting the ground and moving slowly and intently along the ground. Al was sure by Pete's movements that, whatever it was, they didn't know Pete saw them and was stalking them now. Pete had crawled fifty feet ahead of the horses with the big 1861 Henry folded across his arms out in front of him. It wasn't long before Big Al heard the big 1861 Henry bellow out its signature sound, and almost instantly, he heard Pete's yell. "Got 'em!"

They were now riding or, like Al would say, being dragged toward the deer that Pete had shot. Pete was telling Big Al that this deer would provide fresh meat for them for today and the rest of the trip. They would just have to make camp here, make some jerky, and gather more water. Al was thankful for the deer appearing when it did because that gave them a reason to stop without Al having to ask. Big Al would look at anyone like himself as a wimp if he asked to stop, so that would be the last thing he would do, even if it killed him.

The campfire felt very good tonight as they sat around it getting warm while roasting some deer loins and making jerky. They had hobbled the horses so they could graze in the small meadow without being able to run away. It was an old Indian trick in which you would tie a short rope from one front leg to and around the other front leg. This would allow the horses to walk, but they couldn't gallop because they couldn't figure out the how to get their legs in sync. It worked very well unless you got excited and started them running because sometimes then they would accidentally get in sync. *Had to use your head and not blow your cool,* thought Al.

As the two of them were dozing off to sleep, one could hear the cries of the forest around them. Over there was the sound of a wolf pack howling; there were the sounds of a barn owl hooting, of animals walking through the wooded area with branches breaking, and of the running water in the stream nearby. *It is the soothing sounds for God,* thought Pete as he went to sleep. Big Al was listening to the sound too as he dozed off into the night's sleep, and he was thinking of the Indian Great Spirit who had put all the things of the earth here for them to use in a holy way that would not exterminate the plan. They slept like two babies all night long, only waking up for a moment or two from the sounds of the forest around them.

The next morning was overcast with low clouds and a little drizzle in the air. Big Al thought it was perfect weather for catching a cold or pneumonia or something even worse. He was thinking about how lucky he was to have a guy like Pete taking care of him regardless of the time or inconvenience it caused.

They had started out very early this morning. *Way before the chickens would crow,* thought Pete as they rode in silence through the meadows and across the streams. *It is chilly out here, chilly clear to the bone.* His knees were hurting like a tooth gone bad. With this drizzle, the overcast sky, and a slight northwest wind, they would need a big campfire tonight, one that would throw the heat out toward you at twenty feet.

The terrain was getting increasingly steeper and harder to travel on now, with more rocks and ledges to hinder them. Sometimes one of Al's lodgepoles would get caught, and Pete would have to climb down and wiggle it up and down or back and forth to free it again. It was much harder to make much time in their traveling today. One thing that worked out well was, when Al needed to rest and had to stop, Pete would go ahead looking for a small pathway down through all the rocks and cliffs.

Pete had been looking for another pathway down through the steep cliffs for over an hour when, suddenly, there before him stood a bunch of old cedar trees. He was confused as he looked at the used path that led right up to the front of the cedar trees. It was and had been used a lot, but it seemed to go nowhere except into a clump of cedars. Pete dismounted from Old Jim, got down on his knees, crawled underneath the clump, and got the surprise of his life. Behind the clump was an entrance to a big, wide trail that led down the mountainside to a beautiful deep valley down below. Wow, *what a surprise,* thought Pete as he sat there looking at the beauty of it.

Pete was thinking that only he and some of the local Indians would know about this shortcut to the valley below. If he cut a few of the cedars on the backside of the clump just wide enough for the horses to slip through, no one else would know or see this shortcut, and he could use it as long as they stayed around here. *That may be a long time if the train had left him and Big Al behind.* He then started to cut a few of the trees, and within the hour, he was done and was hot and sweaty. He felt good because this would save a lot of time and hassle. Then he mounted Old Jim and hurried back to Al.

Big Al was sleeping when he arrived, so he started a small fire so they could eat something warm and nourishing before hitting the trail hard again. *The small rabbit I have caught when I was looking for the way down the mountainside will be tasty now,* he thought. Al was awake, and they devoured the rabbit in no time flat. Now they were back on the trail and were almost to the spot where Pete had found the hidden trail. They were both excited about this new and faster way to go down the mountainside.

They arrived, and Al had to get off the dragging bed for it to fit between the trees and tree stumps that Pete had left. They lifted it in a couple of places and over the stumps, but they made it. Now they had a nice trail to travel down the mountainside to the settlers' encampment. Both of them were hoping that the wagon train was still there, waiting for them to reappear.

There were only a couple of days now before they would find out the answers to many questions they had. Pete was hoping that Ole had taken charge and was directing the construction of some winter shelters and food storage. Then his thoughts went to Anna. He sure hoped she was okay and was still trusting God to ease her worries. He knew that she always felt better after she prayed long and hard about things, and little did he know about how long and hard she had been praying.

The traveling was going much better on this new trail that Pete had found, which was hidden from the eyes of a would-be passerby. He could tell by the signs in the pathway that this path had been used a lot and for many years by animals and Indians. *The view from this trail looking down over the valley is downright impressive,* thought Pete as he was looking around. It was beautiful and stunning with the color of trees in the fall-shades of green, red, and orange. The clear blue sky overhead was so neat to see along with the rocks covered with moss and, in some places, water running downhill, forming a small stream.

The sights and sounds here in this mountainside hill are amazing, thought Pete as they continued downhill.

Big Al was thinking about the beauty of it all too, but he had been down many trails like this one before, so he was more concerned about his health. He was tired and sore but was keeping his mouth shut so they would reach the wagon train soon. There, he would be taken care of much better than here on the trail, where they didn't have the resources to do a good job on his sores and scars. Al was now thinking about how he must look to an outsider with his big deep scar down his face from years ago and then all the new ones on his shoulders and back. He must look like a practice kit for mountain lions.

Pete pulled up now at the edge of this little stream so the horses could get some water and rest a bit. Both horses drank their fill and then were allowed to go farther out and graze with their hobbles on. Pete did not want to try to catch the horses later; he just wanted to walk up to them and grab the leash, period. And twenty minutes later, he did exactly that; he grabbed the leashes, and they were on their way again.

Now Pete was planning to find a nice, level, and well-protected place to make camp for the night. This camp would be better than most because they may have to stay there for an extra day or two for Al to fully rest up. They would need protection from the northwest wind and also any raiding parties from the various Indian tribes in this area. He would be looking as they went down the mountainside this afternoon. Pete didn't want to get too low on the mountainside for the camp but a spot where they could see all around them, including down below.

About three o'clock in the afternoon, Pete found his spot. Off the trail about a hundred yards was a little overhang with a slight cave-like shape in the rocks that was just enough to get under in case of rain or snow. A campfire would be just on the edge of it where there was a pile of rocks that would block the view of the fire from everyone except the inhabitants of the campsite. Plus, it would reflect the heat back into and toward the camp.

Pete unloaded Big Al and made him comfortable. Then Pete unsaddled Old Jim, put hobbles on him, and turned him out to the small meadow. He also took the pole bed off Al's big horse and turned him out as well. Now he was bringing in firewood that he would use to build the big campfire and also stack a reserve pile for later in the night. *This is a lot of work,* thought Pete.

Al spoke up, saying, "You work like a horse taking care of me, and I ask myself why." Then he continued to say that he wouldn't have taken care of Pete this way. Pete just smiled as Big Al rambled on about this and that. Sometimes Pete thought Big Al talked and talked because, in all the years as a lonely trapper, he didn't have anyone to talk to or with. Pete left the campsite now and was going to look for a rabbit or two for chef's special tonight.

Before too much time had passed, Pete appeared with two rabbits, a clump of wild cabbage, and a couple of onions. *Rabbit stew would be on tonights menu,* he thought as he left the campsite with a bucket for fetching some water from the nearby stream. It wasn't very long before you could smell the stew heating up with a mix of smells coming from the cast-iron pot. Both of the men felt like they could eat everything in the pot by themselves.

This sliding down the trails made a man hungry, thought Big Al as the winds shifted, and the aroma hit his nose.

The sun was shining brightly now as it lowered itself down the skyline on the western side of the valley and mountainside. Pete noticed that, nowadays, the sun was a darker red color just before it went down for the night. He wondered why it was that way. *Good question for God,* he thought. Speaking of God, Pete was thinking of Anna again and was sure that God had watched over her and was her protection too. He was getting excited to see her soon as well as the rest of the people from the train.

Big Al was sound asleep now, and Pete would be soon. *It felt good to rest and talk this afternoon, and Al needs plenty of rest,* thought Pete as he looked at Al. Tomorrow would be another day.

The next morning, Pete and Big Al decided to rest for at least another day. *No hurry now,* thought Pete. *A day or two later wouldn't affect the outcome anyway.*

Over 350 miles away, Oh-y-Yee and the other horses in the pasture were waking up from a long night. It had been windy and cold with some sprinkles in the air most of the night. The herd was grazing in the meadow, walking slowly as they grasped each mouthful of grass, ripping it loose from the ground. It was white clover, and Oh-y-Yee knew that this grass was very powerful. It was high in protein and water content, which meant a horse had to ration the amount that was eaten at one time, or else they would get the grass shits as Awanatu would say.

Today the sun was shining bright, and the wind had died down to five miles per hour. The birds were singing, and the Crow were up and about, doing the normal early morning chores. The young men were preparing to go hunting, and soon they would be coming to get their horses. The middle-aged men were making new weapons like arrows, spears, and hatchets. Shaping the flint rock and making it sharp took one skill, and tying it onto the arrow or spear took another. Each one of them knew what their job was, and they were doing it while talking and laughing about the daily grind. The old men were talking and playing with their youngest grandchildren while the women were making something to eat.

By midmorning, the horses were all lying in the meadow, absorbing the sunshine, with the exception of those selected to go on the hunting party. Awanatu had ten braves with him on horseback when they began climbing up the mountainside to the higher elevation, where they were going to hunt elk. The colder weather was going to bring the elk down from the extremely high elevations to the meadows halfway down the mountainside.

Oh-y-Yee was the lead horse, and she was proud of that fact as she showed almost no effort in jumping up one or two feet when needed in the trail. She was in great shape because of all the Indian war polo games and her trying to show off in front of her friend, the stallion. This hunting trip could be a lot of fun showing the rest of them, plus Awanatu, that she could find and get the elk before the rest of them.

Chapter 9

Three miles up the mountainside, a herd of elk were grazing in the meadow and enjoying the morning sun. The smell in the air was nice and clean like after a heavy rainfall. They were slowly moving along, clipping off the grass as they went, stopping once in a while to look for danger or smell the air for predators. The fall was a nice time high up in the mountains, with the leaves turning colors and the weather changing from hot to cold. The change was always welcome, at least in the first few weeks.

To the east, a few beavers were swimming in their pond while patching the dam and making their hut home ready for winter. Over on the other mountainside, one could hear the howling of a wolf pack to call all of them together for a hunt. It sent a tingle down the backbone of all the animals that the wolves preyed on.

The Crow were taking in all the sounds and watching for movements all along the trail as they moved upward toward where they expected to find the elk. *Tonight we would eat fresh elk meat, and it would melt in our mouths,* thought Awanatu. The whole Crow nation would know his name before long.

Oh-y-Yee could feel the excitement in the way he kicked her sides and handled the reins. She thought he was moving faster than normal too. *This could be my chance to dump him and escape his wrath,* she thought as she continued up the steep incline.

It was about midday when Anna thought again about Al and Pete. She was content now to wait for them and trust God to bring them back. After all, what else could she do? She noticed several things at once like the four men coming into camp with a freshly killed deer and others bringing in more logs for protection, plus firewood. It all seemed so blah to her now when Pete was gone, but before he left, it was exciting. *One thing is for sure,* she thought. *And that is the fact that we are ready for winter.* Ole had done a great job taking Pete's place as the leader of the group.

Pete and Big Al were taking it easy this afternoon, just resting and talking about everything from the day Al first arrived until today. Big Al began talking about his life out here in the Wild West for the first time, and Pete was all ears. When Al was done talking, Pete began thinking about everything he had said.

Al was fifteen years old when he left the East and came out to this part of the West to look for gold but was stranded here without food or money. Then he began hunting for food and shelter, and once that had been accomplished, he discovered he could be a trapper and sell pelts for big money. During the many years he had been trapping, he learned who lived here and who their enemies were. He had learned the language of different tribes and how to work with them or avoid them altogether. He also learned how to trade with them, live with them, and work with them.

Big Al thought that most of the tribes in this area were sent by the Great Spirit in the sky because he was a huge very strong man who brought with him the big thunderstick. They had not seen a white man before or a man this big. Al had played into this whole Indian thought by never appearing weak or simple but strong and smart. He would tell them his power was what made the thunderstick shout so loud.

Pete was thinking that Al must be at least six feet six and three hundred fifty pounds and was naturally very strong. Al looked rough and tough too with the big buckskin coat, long dirty beard, and double set of knives tucked in behind his belt, not to mention his long hair with the feathers tied into the braids and the big scar running down his face. Wow, thought Pete, *what if he had first come here now with the addition of the deep purple scars running down his back?*

After a long silence, Pete said, "Tomorrow we will go down the mountainside more, and by nightfall, we should be close to the valley floor. Then the next day, we should make it back to camp." Al nodded and thought it would be good to get back to camp for some good food and conversation.

The Crow were all excited this afternoon as the hunting party returned with two big bull elk that must have weighed eight hundred pounds each dressed. They had both animals tied up high between two poles, had them gutted, and were cutting off different parts for each family. Most of the meat would be made into jerky, with the rest used up tonight at the feast and dance. It would be good to be in the Crow camp tonight.

Oh-y-Yee was back in the pasture with her friends, running around, free of Awanatu, and kicking up her heels. Some of the horses were rolling in the dust, and some were just lying around, trying to regain their energy. All of them would sleep well tonight.

The old eagle had been flying around today, watching from high above the ground, checking up on all his friends down below. He was now heading back to the big old tree high up on the mountainside to be with his new bride for the night. He would stop when he was closer to the nest and find something to eat and also take some food home for her. The Indians, the settlers, Pete and Al, and all their horses looked good to the old eagle as he flew from camp to camp. He was surprised that Al and Pete were on the move back to the campsite of the settlers. He was thinking it was a fast recovery for Big Al.

As he was nearing home, the old eagle surprised some prairie dogs and had gotten two of them. They were too big to carry home together, so he ate his fill and would then take the other one to his mate. *They are fat and very tasty,* he thought as he flew toward the nest high up on the mountainside.

The next morning was just downright beautiful. A mix of light rain and snow had fallen over the night with mostly rain. Today everything seemed much fresher outside and looked cleaner too. A slight wind was blowing in from the north, but it wasn't as cold as it had been overnight.

Pete was up early and had the fire going high into the air, with hot flames shooting out in all directions. It was talking as the dry pine branches were burning. He had the coffee on the stones next to the fire, and it was enough to keep it hot or hotter than it needed to be. Pete had found a nest of eggs this morning when he was looking for firewood, so he brought them back to camp and was now frying them in his big black frying pan. *Beef jerky, coffee, and now eggs,* he thought, *what more could a guy want?*

Big Al was still sleeping next to the big rock wall of the cave, and his shadow on the rocks behind him was massive to say the least. In their little talks now and then, they had found out a lot about each other and also had learned to respect each other based on their life's story.

Back at the circled wagons, Ole was up and about, looking around to see what else needed to be done before winter, when he started thinking about Pete and Big Al. He was sure they would be coming back at any time as long as the Crow hadn't lifted their scalps. He could use Pete's help now in keeping the peace and planning the daily chores around the encampment. How many logs dragged around the circle were enough? How much dried berries and fruit were enough? How much jerky did they need? The questions continued each day as it got colder and colder. Did he have enough wood piled up for heat for the winter? And then there was the question he was tired of answering: "When will Pete and Big Al come back, or will they?" He wasn't sure anymore how to answer that one because there could be many possible answers.

All the people were up and starting their daily chores now. Ole thought he had a system that worked well as, every day, some things were routine, and others would be added to the to-do list when needed. It was all running smoothly, and he was surprised at the amount of work they could get done in one day. This camp didn't even look close to the original camp that just had the wagons circled. Now they had all the felled trees around the outer borders with log walls at each end of the camp, plus the huge building in the center of the village, the church, and the big root cellar. *The root cellar could also be used as a last-ditch effort if everything else was failing,* thought Ole. That had never occurred to him before, but next summer, they could expand on that if they decided to stay here forever. Ole was becoming too attached, and that also worried him.

Many miles away, the Crow encampment was also up and moving around but slower than everyone else. They had a big dance last night after the hunting trip. All the butchering was completed, and they drank too much of the homemade brew. It was wild berries put into a large container with other fruits and veggies and left undisturbed for days, and then only the top was bled off and kept, and it was fermented again with new berries and herbs for quite a long time until it burned all the way down when swallowed.

Oh-y-Yee was in the meadow grazing with the rest of the herd when she noticed the stallion coming up over the crest of the hill. The picture of him in her eyes made her heart pound hard, and she didn't know why. She pretended she didn't see him whenever he looked her way. She did, though, and the picture of him in her mind never wanted to leave, even when she wanted it to. Oh-y-Yee did not understand this, nor could she figure it out.

It was now midmorning, and the braves of the Crow were finally starting to move around camp slowly. They had more firewater than they realized and had terrible headaches.

The old eagle and his lovely female friend were now flying high in the sky over the Crow nation. They had started early this morning flying west to see what their friends were doing. They were disappointed that the Crow were moving so slow, if at all, and this they did not understand.

It was cooler now than last summer, when the heat rising from the desert floor would lift them thousands of feet in the air without help. Now it was work to fly around, especially after a flight this long. The two eagles flew overhead for a while and then decided to check out Pete and Big Al. So eastward they began. When they had flown for over three hours, they spotted the two guys down below. It appeared to them that Pete and Big Al were staying put for today. It looked peaceful as they headed east again.

It was almost dark when they arrived at the circled wagon train, and the two eagles saw that all was well. Then they both decided to call it a day and headed for home. *We will sleep well tonight,* thought the old eagle as he winged his way home, thinking that this couldn't happen very often. He was hurting.

Now it was several days later, and everyone was starting to move again. Pete and Big Al had been busy this morning breaking camp. That meant putting the packs on the pack mule and the rest of their belongings on their own horses. With Al's horse pulling the tripod with Al lying on it, it really couldn't carry much else, so that meant Old Jim and the mule were elected to do the job.

Pete was thinking it was a good thing that they were traveling in a downward direction. The horses could travel farther and in less time compared with flat or upward climbing. He was not paying attention to where he was going because he had started dreaming about the time they would arrive at the wagon train circle, or at least he hoped the train was still there. What if they had kept going west, or what if the Crow had returned and slaughtered them or they were just gone? His heart was beating faster than normal, and now he started thinking about Anna and how he had missed her throughout all this. Pete was sure that, with him being gone for so long without an explanation of where he was going, it was going to be especially tough on her, and he did not like that feeling at all.

Suddenly, he was brought to his senses by a noise up ahead that sounded like a couple of rifle shots. They would have to find cover, and then he alone would have to go forward and check it out. *Great,* he thought, *more chances of a problem or getting killed or injured without help.* Not only would he be at risk but Big Al too.

Up ahead about a mile and a half, Ole and several men from the train were laughing and excitedly talking about the three big elk they had just shot. All of them had been dropped with only one shot each, and they were fairly close to one another. The men were done skinning the animals and were sitting around in a circle discussing how they should or could pack all the meat and get it back to the train.

Suddenly, they heard the hammer of a rifle move back into a cocking position, and a voice called, "Slowly raise your hands to where I can see them!" They did as they were told. Then the voice said they should turn around slowly or be blown away. When they turned, all of them were totally shocked to see one another.

The men exchanged greetings and howdies when one of them said, "Where is Big Al?" That led to more talking, explaining, and planning.

They decided Pete was going back to get Big Al, and he would take a man named Henk with him to help out. By the time they got back to Big Al, it was time to set up camp for the evening again. Pete was hoping Big Al was awake so Henk could talk to him because it seemed like Al never ran out of things to say, especially after a day when Pete had been gone. He also repeated things many times over.

By the time Ole and the others had the meat all packed onto their packhorses, it was almost dark, and they decided they needed to head for the wagon train. It was slower, but it also was steady, so Ole thought they would arrive shortly after midnight. He couldn't wait to tell Anna that Pete would be home in a couple of days.

The Crow Indians were also preparing for a long and cold winter. They had enough jerky, dried berries, dried fruits, and potatoes but needed more firewood in case the winter was extremely long or cold or both. They were all working very hard on the firewood detail. Men, women, and children were all busy all day long.

Oh-y-Yee and the rest of the herd were enjoying a day off, just grazing and lying around, relaxing. The grass was getting shorter now, so they had to walk farther and longer to get enough to eat. She was thinking about the winter that was coming while she grazed every day. Oh-y-Yee was looking for areas where it was covered with heavy foliage so, when the snow came, she would know where to scrape the ground with her hooves to find dry grass. She also noticed that she had gained a lot of weight this year, but it was in frame and substance, not fat. Oh-y-Yee was by far the biggest strongest female in the Crow nation, and she knew it.

All the braves were tired of collecting firewood every day or helping the women make jerky. They were talking to one another, saying things like "Soon we will be making bows and arrows and preparing for the evil whites that had crossed through our burial grounds." All of them would love the warm fire in the tepee this winter, but now they loved to complain.

At around midnight, Ole and the boys pulled into camp with the load of elk meat. To their surprise, half the people from the wagon train were waiting around the campfire, scared to think of what might have happened to Ole and the group of men. Ole was telling all of them about meeting with Pete out on the mountainside when Anna appeared out of nowhere. He took her to the side and told her the whole story of what had happened to Pete and Big Al. Both of them had tears of joy running down their faces as Ole told all the details that Pete and Al had endured. He said Henk had gone along with Pete to help bring Big Al back to the wagon train. Anna was relieved of all her worries, and now she could hardly wait another day or two.

It did not take much time to unload the meat and hang it in the root cellar for the night with all this help. The talk was going on and on with more questions as the night was thinking of turning into morning. The moon was overhead, and it was full and bright. Ole thought that was a special sign.

Soon everyone was in their wagon, trying to fall asleep. Anna was lying on her back, looking up, and saying over and over again, "Hiank you, thank you, God." She was the last one in camp to fall asleep. Pete, Henk, and Big Al were also fast asleep after much talking and planning about tomorrow.

Hie next morning, Pete was up extra early, making sure the horses had been grazing and watered. Now he was putting the saddles and packs on the horses and loading up. Henk arrived over by the horses and was helping as much as possible. When they had finished, they brought the horses over by Big Al and helped him get into his crib as he called it. Then they started out on the trip.

Big Al and Henk could see the hurried-up attitude of Pete, so they began "giving him shit" about killing Old Jim with the fast pace downhill just to see his "women." Pete was getting a little sick of their fun time at his expense. *But that is life,* he thought. Going downhill was much easier today than ever before because the trail was wide and rock-free. It was because they were on a big flat meadow that covered several hundred acres, and it wouldn't be long before they reached the bottom of the mountain and started down the valley for the wagon train. As he rode along, Pete was also thinking about the Crow and wondered what they were doing now. *Preparing for winter was the most likely.*

Everyone at the campsite was excited today, and they were working very hard to make the campsite look like a city just to impress Pete and the other two when they arrived. They were not sure if it would be today or tomorrow, but they knew it would be soon.

Pete, Henk, and Big Al had now reached the bottom of the mountain and had crossed the stream. They had dismounted and had drank from the stream, and now their horses and the mules were doing the same. They were sitting on the grass on the bank of the stream, talking about when and how far away the wagon train could be, when Pete stated that they should travel down the valley for a couple of hours and then make camp. His reason was that they wouldn't reach camp today anyway, so they might as well take their time and come into camp fresh. They all agreed and went back in the saddle. It was sure hard to take your time like this, but it was best for everyone.

Anna was really excited and was hoping for an early arrival. She kept looking to the west, thinking that at any minute Pete would appear. Ole caught himself doing the same thing as did others in the train.

Pete was thinking about Big Al, and he was sure that the mountain man would be walking around soon. He had noticed a big improvement lately. Big Al was also thinking about the last few months and how he had wondered many times if he would live or die. Once he knew the answer, he started to think if he would ever walk again. Now he was sure he would do both.

Many hundred miles away, the Crow nation was all ready for winter with plenty of buffalo jerky prepared along with many dried fruits and nuts. They had been working extra-long days preparing because, last year, they had not readied enough food for a tough long winter. And it was. White Buffalo was the oldest Crow in camp, and he had never seen a winter like the last one. He was afraid they may starve to death before it was over, so he had been preaching all summer long to gather more fruit, berries, and jerky before the first sign of Old Man Winter. And that was what they did.

Winter was closing in all across the northern Plains of Colorado and Utah. Everyone was either ready for it or preparing for the dreaded part of the year. This was way before electric lights, flashlights, running water, and woodstoves. Your camp needed to be close to running water from a spring or stream because still water would freeze solid. Many of today's comforts were not even thought of, let alone made. Most of the things needed to make the winter bearable needed to be planned well ahead of time. You could not just "turn up the heat." You had to bring in the firewood and start a small fire, which would take an hour to be heated and another hour before your cabin or tepee was warm. This was possible only if you had gathered firewood in the fall and if it was seasoned. Seasoned firewood was wood that had been dead or cut a year ago so that it was now dry. Many of the things needed took this slow to be made usable.

Today Awanatu was putting sod around the edge of his tepee for two reasons. It would keep the water out and seal the sidewalls of the tepee so the cold air could not blow under the sides and make all the heat go out through the hole in the roof made for the smoke to escape. He was lucky because he was of high rank; therefore, he could have a much bigger tepee than most of the braves. His also had pictures painted on the sides showing Oh-y-Yee and himself in war. Her picture was beautiful with the dreaded sign of the hand on her rump. Every time he entered the tepee, he would look at the painting and smile. He was a proud man, and he was also proud of his famous horse, Oh-y-Yee.

On the inside, he had several quivers full of arrows hanging down from the side of the tepee, and each quiver had a bow with it. He also had a U.S. saber attached to one of the lodgepoles and a Colt repeating carbine close by. He also had several shields made from cured and stretched buffalo hides, which were strong enough to stop a bullet from a medium-sized rifle. There were antlers, rocks, and equipment for making more weapons lying off to one side. The bed was made by putting down a bunch of pine boughs first and then lying a big buffalo robe over them. In the center of the tepee was a fire circle about five feet across, bordered with stones that were like granite so they would hold the heat longer than normal.

Around the campsite were several big firepits that always had a fire burning in them. This provided light and heat for the guard at night and also on cold days. There was a distinct smell in the air that made it cozy, and it was the burning of pine needles and branches. It also sounded cozy with the dry wood crackling when a lump of sap hit the open flame. To the average human, the smell, the fire's heat, and the light from it were all transformed into security. It was all good.

Oh-y-Yee was on the outskirts of the encampment, looking toward it and thinking to herself. She was wondering why winter had to come every year and bring with it the cold north wind, snow, and ice. It always meant that dry grass under the snow would be hard to find; plus, it would not taste like the lush grass of the meadows in the springtime. Maybe it was because the Great Spirit wanted every living thing to be thankful for what they had and not cry or complain when they did not need to. *It seems to work that way most of the time,* she thought as she continued to think of the times of shortages when any old blade of grass was great to eat. *The Great Spirit keeps us in his hand and feeds us each day, and he makes us strong by making us work for it.* It made sense to her after thinking about it for a few minutes.

The old eagle and his friend were staying in the nest this winter more than normal. It was cold already, and soon the snow would be very deep, and it would be hard to find mice and other small field animals to feed him and his young friend. Then they would have to depend on their keen eyesight to find other animals that had not survived the hard cold weather.

Chapter 10

On another cliff overlooking the valley below from the south side stood a stranger. He was tall and strong and looked like he had traveled for a long time without much rest. He was sixteen and a half hands high and dark cherry red with a white stripe down his face and one white sock on his rear right leg. Yes, he had been ridden long and hard. He was needing rest too. A stallion he was and impressive to look at as well.

This stallion just knew how to work long and hard without ever fighting back against his owner's demands, even though at times the demands were severe. The stallions name was Shadow. He was used to the hard long days on the trail and knew just about when his master would call for a rest. As a matter of fact, that was how he received his name, by being where he was supposed to be when the master expected him.

The man up on the big stallion had rough features that looked windburned and wrinkled. He appeared to be in his late forties or early fifties, but the outdoors could change the appearance of a man in just a few short years. Who knows how many years this man had been outdoors in the wild frontier? He was a tall, lean man who looked to be made of dried sinew and hard muscles from the weather and plenty of hard work.

He was wearing a long leather raincoat and fancy-decorated tall boots. His shirt appeared to be of the finest buckskin, and his pants matched the shirt. Under the jacket, there appeared to be a holster with double Colt 45s in it. His man was ready and willing to have a fight with someone. Who was he looking for and why? was the question.

Shadow had a very expensive saddle on his back that had all the extras. There was fancy leather work with designs of cowboys and horses throughout. A big scabbard for a very big rifle hung on the right side of the saddle on Shadow, and another held a knife that looked more like a sword. On the left side was a special holster for a Colt .45 with a long barrel. This man was armed to the teeth.

Ron stepped down off Shadow. He was six feet and six inches, two hundred forty-five pounds with wide shoulders and strong arms. This man was not one that you would want to tangle with day or night.

Off in the brush fifty feet from the edge of the cliff, there were two packhorses loaded with supplies and extra clothing. Who was this man? Was he a bounty hunter, a lawman looking for outlaws, a loner, or an outlaw who robbed banks and rich frontiersmen, like the group of Norwegian frontiersmen in the wagon train circled below?

Just then, the old eagle flew overhead, and he noticed the stranger in the neighborhood. *Who is that?* he wondered as he flew toward his nest. *And why is he here? I guess* we *will find out later.* And he worked his way home.

Down in the valley below, everyone was waking up from a night's sleep. Pete had the coffee going over the open flames of the campfire, and it had a nice aroma this morning better than most. He also had his old skillet over the flames with some pancakes baking slowly inside it. He was thinking about later today when they would arrive at the wagon train. Wow, he thought, *we have been gone a long time.*

Big Al was lying in his buffalo robe, pretending to be sleeping as he listened to Pete whistle the song "The Old Rugged Cross." He wanted to jump up and scare Pete and give him some shit about his singing, but it was pretty good. Plus, it was a hymn, so it wouldn't be in good taste. About the time the flapjacks were ready, Big Al decided to show that he was alive and hungry. Pete was ready for him with a plateful ready along with some beef jerky. They all ate like there would never be another meal, and it was very good.

In another half hour, they were starting to saddle up and get the packhorses loaded. Things couldn't move fast enough for Pete, and the other two thought it was moving way too fast. The people of the wagon train were starting their day out too. Fires were roaring and smells of coffee and smoke in the air along with a strong smell of bacon.

Anna was worried again, thinking it had been a few days ago when she expected to see Pete again, and she didn't know when or even if he was coming now. What if something had gone wrong again and someone was hurt or, worse yet, killed? She tried to be positive but just couldn't be right now. The stress was getting her down.

Ole was thinking that if the boys didn't show up today, he would send a search party out looking for them tomorrow. His confidence was also at an all-time low. He was sure he had everyone and everything prepared for winter, but he kept doubting his ability.

The campsite had grown and was much better for them now than before. *The big stockade at each end of the encampment is a huge improvement for protection,* he thought as he stood silently off to the side of the group, not to mention the trees that had been dragged along the sides of the camp. The community building in the center of town was also impressive along with the huge root cellar.

At about three in the afternoon, Anna heard someone shouting at the west end of the campsite, and then more people were shouting, and it was getting louder and louder. Her heart was leaping inside as she started running toward the west side. *Could that be the boys?* she thought. Anna was almost afraid to look as she neared the west end of the camp, but she did, and there one hundred yards out were three riders and a couple of packhorses or mules. Instantly, she saw Pete in the saddle on Old Jim. Before she realized it, she was fifty feet ahead of everyone, running toward the horses and the men.

Pete had goosed Old Jim, and they were running toward the group. It wasn't long before they were all hugging one another and talking faster than the person next to them and even trying to be louder. This would continue well into the night tonight.

Ron had spotted Pete and his group about six or seven miles back down the valley. He had made sure no one had spotted him as he followed them from high up on the mountainside inside the tree line. Ron was wondering where three men with a couple of packhorses were going with one of them injured so badly that he needed a sling behind his horse. Now he had found out where they were going, so now he had to think some more about these men and their wagon train. He pulled Shadow farther to the right up into the trees to look for a place with water where he could set up camp. It was cold out, and pretty soon snow would be falling, and Old Man Winter would be here in force.

Everyone at the circled encampment was talking and helping prepare a big party for the evening with a fancy meal and a big thank-you to God for bringing the boys home safely. The talking was nonstop as everyone was sharing the news of what had happened with both groups. No one even noticed the weather was changing quickly.

The wind was blowing hard out of the northwest at about thirty-five miles per hour. Early in the day, it had been fifty-five degrees, but now it was only thirty. It was still dropping about five degrees per hour. It would be cold tonight, and they had better be ready because it may stay cold until spring now.

Around midnight, it started, and it rained cats and dogs for several hours, and then it turned to snow. Ole was up, checking the water levels of the creek beside the circled wagons. He was concerned that they might be flooded in the morning. *But,* he thought, *it is good to see it this cold because that will stop the runoff, preventing the flooding.*

The party had continued late into the night, with everyone exchanging stories about what had happened to each of them. Many of the people in the wagon train had asked all about the ordeal with the big cat attacking Big Al but had forgotten about the Crow Indians. Suddenly, Ole jumped to his feet and began asking fourteen questions at the same time about the dreaded Crow. Had they seen them, or had they seen signs of them? Were they still in the area? Everyone was getting excited about the news that was going to come from Pete as soon as he could rise to his feet.

Pete started out by calming them down, stating that they had not even seen a trace of the Crow, let alone any of them. He was sure they had gone all the way back to Utah or Idaho for their winter campsites. When he finished telling all that he knew about the subject, he suggested they all turn in for the night. And that was what they did.

The next morning, five hundred miles to the west and northwest, the Crow nation was waking up to a howling wind that was blowing very hard from the north. It was fifteen degrees below zero, and it was snowing a lot and had done so for several hours. Hie snow had already reached one foot up from the ground, and the wind was making huge drifts here and there along the path. Hie campfires were burning very hot and fast with the extreme wind, so the tribal leaders decided to only keep one big fire outside and move the rest inside the tepees. Awanatu had looked outside for only a moment and thought about how lucky he was to have prepared the night before by placing a lot of wood inside his tepee. Now he could stay inside where it was warm, eat some buffalo jerky, and make some more arrows for the upcoming war with the whites in the wagon train.

All the Indian ponies were hiding down in a ravine where the braves had put them the previous night. Hie wind was howling overhead, and the snow was blowing, but down in the ravine, it was peaceful and not very bad at all. Oh-y-Yee thought that these Indians were pretty clever to have figured this out. Her hair had grown long this past fall, and at times, she seemed very warm, but now she felt very comfortable when she was out of the direct wind. She wondered how long this storm would last. If she remembered correctly, most of them were over in a couple of hours; but once in a while, one would last for twenty-four hours, and they were hard to take. One would get very hungry by the time one could go back to the meadow and paw for grass under the snow. With a strong, cold wind, thirst would set in, in a few hours. Hiat was another reason why the ravine was a good idea because it had a small stream running through it. It would not freeze because of the speed of which it ran.

The storm was moving fast across the Plains and would soon hit Kansas. It was going to be the first storm of the year and maybe the largest. It was blowing very hard across the northern Plains this morning. It had snowed very hard all night, and it was still snowing at a record pace. The problem now was that the wind had picked up to a howling forty miles per hour and was expected to do so all day long. Last night's snow was drifting, and the new one was only making it deeper. If it kept blowing and snowing, it would be hard on everyone and everything in its path. Everything would need to find shelter one way or another.

By midafternoon all across the northern Plains, everyone and all the animals had found a shelter of some kind; and if they hadn't, they would most likely die. The Crow had found shelter in their tepees. The settlers found shelter inside their wagons or in the big building at the center of the campsite. All the horses from both groups were in deep ravines, where they were protected from the strong winds and the cold air that seemed to go straight through one's body. The old eagle and his friend were in their nest, buried down in the deepest part, trying to stay out of the wind. The big, tall stranger had also found a cave in the side of the mountain, and it was big enough for both him and Shadow to fit inside with room to spare. All the people were in tepees, the community building, or covered wagons. The horses were all in different ravines protected from the storm. Every one of them was getting hungry, but no one dared to go outside during a storm like this.

In a blizzard like this with high wind, you would become disoriented and lost within twenty feet after leaving your shelter, so no one tried to leave. But why would you want to leave? The fire was burning hot, and the sound of wood crackling was peaceful. The temperature was now at negative forty-three degrees. The wind had died down, but it had left fifteen-foot-high drifts everywhere. In a few hours, everyone would have to start digging out from under the deep snow. This would be a major job in itself.

The next morning, Oh-y-Yee and her herd mates were all out in the big meadow near the Crow encampment. It was very cold, but the wind had died down to almost nothing. She thought it felt 100 percent better than yesterday, but finding dead grass under the deep snow was extremely hard work. *This is going to be a long winter,* she thought as she continued to paw for more of the dead grass. Oh-y-Yee was glad she was a little plump because pawing for a mouthful of dead grass was not going to keep her in good condition for very long. She loved the days right after a big storm because they always felt warmer than normal, and the air was cleaner. Her herd mates had learned to spread out far and wide to find more dead grass quicker.

Over two hours later, she noticed the Crow were starting to move about, lighting the big campfires and preparing for the day. Oh-y-Yee knew she would not have to work for a while because the deep snow would make hunting easier for the Crow on foot. They could track the animals in the snow and then run them into the deep snow for the easy kill shot. The older buffalo would be slower; plus, the deep snow would make them even slower. The extreme cold would also help keep the meat longer before it had to be made into jerky. Hie Crow would be enjoying fresh meat every day now for a while, with their big stew pots boiling all day long with meat scraps, carrots, potatoes, and other veggies. This was a good time to be a Crow.

Oh-y-Yee thought the Crow had it made until she remembered the long summer's heat when they ate nothing but jerky. In the summertime, the horses had it made with shade and lush long dark green grass that filled the meadows. The Crow would be making and eating dried jerky all summer long, which she compared with eating the dead dry grass of winter. Now with her belly full of dry grass, she lay down and was almost instantly asleep.

She started dreaming of next spring when all the horses had shed off their long and ugly winter's hair. The Crow would take them to a new meadow every day to ensure the best grasses were eaten for rapid weight gain. They would also start working them a little harder each day until they were ready for the long haul of the warpath. The Crow were excellent with horses and knew how far they could push them. They would start with war games and running up and down the trails nearby. That would be expanded until the horses could run five or six miles and then walk for two, and then they would continue running for another five or six miles. After a couple of months, they would be able to do this all day long without getting tired. Oh-y-Yee dreaded those first two months, but after that, she thought it was fun. Her reason for liking it was that no other horse could run as long or as fast as she could. Something about being the best was fun.

The dream continued with many war games, and in each one, she and Awanatu won many scalps. We *are the best anywhere,* she thought. And they were. Then they were on a long journey to the east, and in a haze, she could see a campsite with many horses, wagons, children, and men. Awanatu and the other Crow braves were sneaking through the forest, watching intently on the campsite down below near the stream. Suddenly, a loud shout aborted her dream, and she awoke to see Awanatu standing there with a carrot. That was her favorite food in all the world. This dream would be continued later.

She and Awanatu had a great day together. He brushed her most of the morning with his hand-carved comb made from hickory wood. It felt so good to be pampered. She had almost forgotten how good it felt. Awanatu was glad to see that Oh-y-Yee was overweight because that meant she could handle a long, cold, and tough winter. And he was afraid it was going to be just that.

While standing there being brushed, she thought about the day she would be able to get rid of Awanatu. She had tried many times, but he was an excellent rider who seemed to know how to handle every twist and turn she put on him. Rubbing him off on a low-hanging branch while riding at a full gallop had been tried and failed. But she wanted it more severe than something that simple; she wanted him to be hurt badly. Oh- y-Yee wanted to leave him far away out on a lonely trail by himself, so if nothing else worked correctly, he would at least have a long way to walk to get home. *Injured would be best,* she thought. *And that would repay him for all the beatings he had given me in the beginning of their relationship.*

Winter had set in all across the Plains now. It was very cold with a lot of snow, wind, and ice. Pete was very impressed with the way Ole had prepared the settlers and the settlement for winter. They had an enormous amount of food stored in the root cellar, with everything from potatoes and carrots to hanging buffalo and jerky made from deer and elk. Outside the community building and along the eastern side, he had firewood stacked as high as the building for the entire length. Ole even had a stack of prairie grass at the end of the encampment. Pete thought that Ole did everything at least as good as he would have done it. He was impressed. It looked like winter would not be bad here.

The campsite was good up here on this little rise in the ground because it would allow the creek to be over its banks and still not run into the campsite. The little rise was also very close to the stream and protected on the north side by the tall mountains on the other side of the creek. The wind was not bad here because of the mountains, and that had made the snow carry farther out to the outer edge of the camp and fill in by the downed trees to make a super barrier. Pete thought it would be almost impossible to attack from any side now during the winter. The snow had filled in the felled trees, making a natural barrier over ten feet tall. *Impressive,* he thought again and again, *and well designed.*

A week and a half went by very slowly as the cold weather, wind, and snow continued. But today it was warmer without the wind, and the sun was shining bright. It was the first chance Pete had to walk the entire campsite, inspecting it as he went. The big building at the center of camp was very impressive. He thought the people must have given it all they could during the time he was gone. They must have worked long hours and very hard to build it so big and correct. It looked stately. Heavy logs that were hand-planed, two-by-ten flooring with four-by-twelve ceiling beams, heavy window and door frames with hand-carved railings going up to the second floor—it was stately and impressive. *The rest of the campsite is very well constructed and planned out too,* thought Pete. *Very good.*

High up in the mountains on the southern side of the wagon train sat Ron in the opening of the cave he had found during the last large rainfall. He had a roaring fire burning behind him that was pushing the heat toward the front opening of the cave. *It really feels good to have the heat forcing its way through your body when it is so blasted cold outside,* he thought. He had carried many loads of dried wood into the cave in the last four weeks and even had his horse helping.

The big and powerful stallion named Shadow did not especially like being used as a pack mule, but he had learned that it was better than lying around the meadow with hobbles on, wondering what Ron was doing. Plus, he also helped carry in many loads of dry hay that would sure be better than pawing the ground, trying to the find grass under the snow. Shadow was now standing toward the back of the cave, chewing a clump of very good-tasting clover hay. He was wondering why they had stopped here when, in other years, they would have continued south until they hit warmer weather.

Ron continued to skin the three rabbits he had killed this morning. When he finished cooking them, he was planning on making moccasins to wear on the insides of his fancy big cowboy boots. That would keep him warmer than ever for the whole winter season. A man always needed something to do too. Ron's thoughts were starting to wander as he sat skinning the bunnies. *Should I stay in this area or ride on?* he though. *Or should I follow the wagon train I have spotted? Maybe the train is not going to move either.* He was wondering who was hiding on that train. Ron thought he would have to watch them for a while to see who and what they were.

The snow was coming down faster than ever right now, and the temperature felt much warmer than earlier in the day. He was done scraping the skins and had dried them and now was sewing them together for moccasins. *Peaceful,* he thought as he watched the snow fall for a minute. Little did he know about the future as it was to change big time.

The old eagle and his newfound lover were enjoying the snowfall from their nest high up on the mountainside and in the big pine tree that had stood in that spot for over 140 years. They enjoyed being there a lot this winter. He was thinking that they had lost track of time now and had not checked up on anyone down below for a long time. One of these days, they would have to go scouting again.

The Crow had been hiding in their campsite as much as possible too. The winter had been harsh so far, and everyone seemed to be enjoying a warm fire with good food. Oh-y-Yee and her friends were always digging for grass under the snow when the weather was good and hiding in the ravines when it was cold and windy. *Soon,* she thought, *spring would come as quickly as a thief during the night and surprise us. I had better run around each day to stay in shape, or it would be rough on me later.* Her mane was long, and her body hair was real long, protecting her from the cold winter. Oh-y-Yee knew that when spring came, she would be ridden hard along with the rest of the horses to find the palefaces back toward the east to avenge their march through the burial grounds.

This afternoon, Ron saddled Shadow, and they headed out from their cave to a southeastern direction. The snow was deeper than expected, and the going was extremely slow. After an hour of traveling, they came to a small stream that was still open and not frozen over like a slow-moving stream would be. They drank some of the ice-cold water, crossed the stream, and headed almost straight east up through a thicket of young jasper pines. After a few minutes, they leveled off from the upward climb and came to a small meadow with many small berry bushes around the edges. Ron stopped the horse, looked to all directions, and then looked again. It was like he expected something or someone to be there, and they may not be friendly.

Ron stepped down off Shadow, looked around, and then pulled the big buffalo gun from the scabbard that was attached to the saddle. He made sure it was loaded, tied the reins to a small group of berry bushes, and walked off to the northeast. The snow was deep here, and Shadow watched as Ron crept toward a small hill crest just thirty feet away from where he had dismounted. He was now crawling in the snow and was planning on doing so until he reached the crest. When he did, he carefully looked over the top and saw a huge buck white-tailed deer. The rifle seemed to come into focus by itself, took aim, and fired. The big buffalo gun sounded like a cannon blast and echoed several times before it was quiet again. The buck lay in the snow with a hole through the chest cavity big enough for your fist to go through it. Ron ran to the buck and started to gut and skin him while thinking about having a fresh steak tonight.

Ole and his group of men from the wagon train stopped in their tracks when the sound of the big gun reached them. They knew it was a big 1860 or '61 buffalo gun. But they all knew that Pete was the only one in these parts to have one of them. Who could this be? Where was he? What was he doing out here? They sat down and listened more intently.

Two hours later, Ron had finished cutting the buck into pieces, had the meat wrapped inside the hide, and had the deer hide up and over Shadow's back. Now he started walking on the trail they had made when they came here to go back toward the cave. It was going to be dark when they got back. He would rub down the horse after unloading all the meat, water him, and tie him in the back of the cave with some fresh hay. Then he would cover the deer meat with snow to cool it overnight. And he would roast a big steak himself.

Ole and the men listened for about an hour and a half before they continued about their business. But they were aware that they had company in the area. This fact bothered Ole. Who was it out here this time of the year? The group had also bagged a big buck with a couple of elk earlier in the day. All the way back to the wagon train, they talked about the gunfire they had heard today and continued to wonder who it was.

This morning, the sun was up early because of the lack of clouds in the sky. Ron thought it felt twenty degrees warmer than yesterday, even though it was only five degrees warmer. *No wind, no clouds, and no cold, perfect,* he thought when his mind wandered off to yesterday afternoon. He just had this feeling like someone else was in the area and was looking for him. He thought for a moment about it and then returned to cutting the meat and drying it over the open fire, thus making jerky. It sure smelled good in the cave and directly outside it. He hoped no one was looking for him today because the smell of drying beef jerky would carry for miles.

The wagon train, down in the valley, was very busy too. They had started early in cutting meat and preparing it for the fire and the jerky process. Ole had thought he could smell jerky being made as he came back into camp from taking care of the horses, but when he arrived, they just had a big roaring fire going. His thoughts started to swirl around to the sound of the big buffalo gun blast from yesterday by wondering who that was and what were they doing up here in the mountains in the wintertime. He was thinking that there could only be one, two, or three of them simply because of a lack of shelter and continued food supply. It was early in the winter, so did that mean that they were caught by surprise? Were they trying to get through the mountains late in the year, or were they looking for a place to settle down? The more he thought about it, the more convinced he was that it was a fur trapper or an outlaw. *We may have to he more alert,* Ole thought as he neared Pete and Big Al.

Anna was busy with the other ladies, helping turn the lard into soap and cooking oils while chatting about this or that. She was so happy now that Pete was back in camp with Big Al. *They have become best friends,* she thought as she looked toward them and smiled.

Many of the children were playing in the snow, making snowmen and such. It was beautiful today. The older ones were helping with the meat and jerky while stealing a piece now and then.

Ron had the last of the jerky on the fire now and was thinking about taking Shadow out for a look around to see if anything was new nearby. He had this nervous feeling about yesterday's hunt, and it had its effects on his actions today. He was bothered by the blast of the big gun and wondered for how many miles the blast was heard and who heard it. In a short time, the jerky was cured, and he saddled Shadow and rode out in the direction of yesterday's hunt.

In about forty-five minutes, they arrived at the site of the killing without any sign of anyone. He thought he had better ride out in a big circle, and each time he came around, he would make the circle bigger until he was convinced one way or the other that someone heard the big gun. After the first big circle yielded nothing, they started the second one and then the third one and so on. About four hours later, he found many hoofprints in the snow, with some of them being pack animals, and they were carrying a heavy load. *This is odd,* he thought. *This means the riders on the horses are looking for something or someone. Otherwise, they wouldn't drag packhorses way up here with a heavy load on them.*

Ron nudged Shadow, and they started to follow the new trail of hoofprints around corners, over hilltops, and down through streams of water until they came to a little clearing at the edge of the mountains where he could see the valley below. He could see the village on the far side of the valley with everyone working with the fresh kill. *Who are they, and why are they here?* he wondered.

They are easy to find, he thought. *So that means I would be easy to find also, if anyone cares.* He would need to protect his location better until he knew who he was dealing with right now. Ron was riding back toward camp now and was thinking about everything that surrounded his camp. The location was great, high up on the side of the mountain and just far enough back from the edge of the cliff, so no one could see the cave from below. You had to stumble into it to know it was there at all. For this, he was happy.

On the way back, he decided to go much farther west past the cave before heading back toward it. He came up through some thickly planted cedar trees and around a small hill before sneaking through a thicket of wild berry plants to the front of the cave. *This will be my new entrance,* he thought. It would be less likely found by accident. He felt much safer and secure now that he had found this pathway to the cave. He started to build a fire and then realized what a pain in the ass the new trail was for bringing in firewood. *Oh well, that is what I need to be hidden up here in the mountains.*

Shadow had been watered and fed some dry grass that Ron had stored in the back of the cave. Ron was finishing washing the plate and pan that he had used when he ate some stew this evening. He was going to roll out his blanket over the pine boughs now and call it a day.

As the sun was setting in the west, clouds were rolling in from the northwest. Ron knew that tomorrow would be different from today. The snow would be coming, followed by a strong wind that would send each little grain of snow into another, blowing them along until something stopped them or shielded them from the wind. *The drifts will be high in some spots tomorrow,* thought Ron.

Chapter 11

The next morning, the drift in front of the cave was ten feet high and had made a perfect curved fence all along the front of the cave. It had made the cave feel warm and cozy, with the big fire roaring inside the entrance. During the night, Shadow had moved closer to the inside than the outside. It looked like they would be stuck here today.

Over fourteen miles away, Ole and the wagon train people were starting to "shovel out" from the big snowstorm. The fires had been started and were roaring away, with the sparks flying skyward. Soon the women and children would be making something to eat while the men would be feeding the horses and cows. Some would be gathering milk, eggs, and other foods out of the root cellar.

All of a sudden, Ole thought about the stranger up in the mountains to the south, wondering who he was and why he was here. When Pete walked up behind Ole, he did not hear him until Pete said, "Good morning."

Ole jumped halfway out of his skin and then did it again for no reason at all. Once he had gathered his wits about him, he asked Pete, "Who do you think the stranger in the forest above the wagon train to the south was, and what is he doing here?"

Pete shook his head as if to say he didn't know. After a while, Pete told Ole not to worry about it because he was only one man, and they were a bunch. Pete didn't want everyone in the camp running scared over nothing. *Time would tell,* he thought as he walked toward the big building in the center of town.

Six hundred fifty miles to the west and slightly north, the Crow nation was also waking up and finding a lot of new snow on the ground.

Awanatu thought about all the snow and drifts around and knew that spring would be late this year. That also meant that it would take longer to get the horses and braves into fighting shape. He was ready to avenge the dead from the whites who had crossed through the holy burial grounds last year. Scalps needed to be on each lodgepole in the entire encampment along with a memory of the palefaces dying a horrible death. That was what he wanted more now than ever, and he was going to make sure it was done this year. He would start next week with braves working the horses to get everyone in shape.

Awanatu would also call for a big war dance and feast as soon as he felt they were ready. If the Crow started early in the spring riding east to find the palefaces, it would be more of a surprise than meeting them somewhere in June or July, when they could hunt and camp easily. Maybe they should even leave here while the snow was on the ground. He would have to give this more thought.

Oh-y-Yee could see Awanatu strolling about all morning, and she was sure that he was now restless. *Hard training would start soon,* she thought. *All that running up the hills and back down just to go up again time after time, what a drag!* She decided that this would be the year that she taught him a lesson about who the boss was in this tribe. With that, she raced around the meadow for a few minutes, trying to get some action in her legs other than stiffness.

This winter has seemed cold and harsh compared with many others, thought Oh-y-Yee as she watched the other horses scratching and pawing for dry grass underneath the snow. A lot of wind and cold coming from the northwest made it seem colder and longer. It was lucky that last year had plenty of rainwater, so the grass had grown way taller than the average year. She also started to paw for food.

Her coat was now very thick with a heavy undercoat, and the hair on the outercoat was twice as long as normal too. The outercoat acted like shingles on a house, causing the rain to run off her to keep the undercoat dry and her body temperature normal. It also kept the wind out. Oh-y-Yee felt like the extra hair made her look fat and unattractive, but Awanatu thought it made her look strong and stout.

After several hours of pawing the ground, most of the horses in the Crow nation had enough dry grass to fulfill their needs for another day.

Then one by one, they headed to the nearest stream to get a full tummy of water. It had to be drank slowly this time of the year because it was just warmer than ice. Too much, and your throat would freeze and thaw, and then you would catch a cold and get sick. Besides, there wasn't much else to do, so you might as well hang out by the stream chatting. This stream was down in a ravine, so it also felt good because it protected each horse from the strong wind when it was blowing.

All through the camp, quivers were full of new sharp arrows, and leaning on the lodgepoles were well-oiled carbines. Most of the carbines were the Army .44-caliber repeating rifles that the Crow had stolen from the battlefield on different years. Piles of bullets were in bowls around the poles, and several spears and tomahawks were there as well. Shields made of stretched buffalo hides were hanging and curing on the outer walls of the tepees. It appeared that everyone in camp was ready for war, and they were just waiting for the spring rains to come.

The fires were roaring in the tepees today because it was so cold outside. Many of the people had not even looked outside unless they needed more firewood. They were busy sewing and making new bows, more arrows, or tomahawks. It took a lot of time to shape a stone into an arrowhead and then fasten it to the arrow shaft. They needed to use leather that had not dried yet because they wanted the leather to shrink and hold the arrowhead to the shaft tightly as it dried. The same was done with the spears and the bows. It all took time, and they had plenty of that now. Some of the older folks were making clay pots and bowls because today the tepee would be very hot, and they could use that to their advantage for curing the clay into a smooth glasslike surface.

Oh-y-Yee was resting with the rest of the herd now down by the stream in the ravine. She started thinking about the young stallion from last fall that had caught her eye when she realized that she couldn't even remember his name anymore. Wow, *I thought I will never forget him, but I have.* The wind was blowing hard overhead now, and she was glad they had stayed down here for the night.

All across the Plains, the animals and humans had bedded down for the night, being thankful they had shelter and heat or protection of some kind. Ron and Shadow were deep back into the cave. The old eagle and his mate were snuggled deep down in the nest. The wagon train's people were in their wagons, wrapped in many blankets. And the Crow were in their tepees with the best warm air of all, but that would also make tomorrow seem colder.

Awanatu did not care about tomorrow; he was happy about today. *Soon,* he thought, we *will start training for the palefaces that had disrespected our ancestors holy grave sites.* In a little while, his thoughts turned into dreaming about the way he would fight when he found them. That dream continued all night long, and it made him restless. He talked in his sleep about what he would do to them when he found the palefaces. His dream told him he was the best brave the Crow had ever had. Oh-y-Yee was also dreaming, but she was thinking about the lush green meadows that would appear soon and the fun of running around the meadow, acting like she didn't want to be noticed for her style or form when she really wanted to show off to everyone everywhere.

It was midnight, and all dreams had stopped for tonight, and only snoring and coughing were heard. The moon was out bright and shiny, making the snow look like fine ice all over the ground. It was getting very cold fast.

Ron woke up this morning and just lay there looking up skyward, wondering if it was March yet. It was quite a few days into the winter as the days were noticeably getting longer now. The cold winter wind was still here along with big snowstorms, but some days were warmer and sunnier than a few weeks ago. Ron thought that you just knew it was changing if you were out in it long enough throughout your life. Little signs included a small melting of snow on the ridges of a drift, more singing by the birds around you during the day, or a small growth at the end of the evergreen branches. The smell in the air was slightly different too.

Now the smoke was giving off its aronia on a still, quiet morning high overhead of the entrance to the cave when Ron thought about it. He panicked a little bit when he wondered if anyone was out there looking for him and thinking about the tall column of smoke going high into the sky. *Surely, it will lead right to my front door,* he thought. Hiat bothered him.

About fifteen miles away, Ole and a group of men from the wagon train saw it too. They were to the northwest of it, looking toward the valley. *On the way back to the wagon train, we will be looking for this place where the smoke is rising slowly,* thought Ole. But it might be across the valley and up the other side of the mountains, and if that was so, they would look some other time.

Ron had Shadow saddled now when he kicked snow over the lire to stop the smoke signal that was going high into the sky. He thought it was like a big finger pointing straight down from above, saying, *Here he is.* Now he was riding to the west to see what was in that direction.

Hie old eagle and his young lover were flying high over the valley below today. It was warmer than it had been for quite some time, and the hot air currents were back, allowing them to flow high freely in the sky. They just spread their wings and held them out while the wind carried them up and down and back up again, giving them excitement.

Hie old bird noticed the stranger riding his horse on the south side of the valley, west of the wagon train, and he wondered who he was, what he was doing here at this time of the year, and where he had been until now in this high country. Everyone knew that he didn't just appear high up in the mountains this time of the year; he had to have been here before the first snowstorms, but where had he been hiding? The old eagle decided they should just follow his trail backward to see who he was or at least where he came from.

Pete and Big Al were standing out in the middle of the town square when Pete noticed the old eagle and his lady flying overhead. He looked at Big Al and said he thought that was the same old eagle that had been here all along. Al chuckled and said, "Sure it was," just to avoid a confrontation.

Then Anna appeared with the two of them and said, "Isn't that the same old eagle that was here when we first stopped to make camp?" Both guys started to laugh as Anna wondered why.

There it was, that sparkle of something shiny, like the first time he flew over the wagon train. Now he stared down at it, and he could make out a cross covered with diamonds. The eagle remembered that the lady who wore it always grabbed it when she was worried or concerned. And there was a difference between worried and concerned, which the old eagle could tell by the way she grabbed it. It had been a long time since the old eagle had seen her, but he was glad she was alive and doing well because he had grown to love her tender and loving heart.

The old eagle and his young friend were flying high over the wagon train when they decided to fly toward home. It was getting later in the afternoon when they arrived at the big nest in the tall tree high on the mountainside. It felt good to have his feet down in the warm nest with his girlfriend next to him, fitting tightly into the nest to seal it up around the edges, making it very warm at the bottom.

Night was coming very fast now. With the clear sky, the stars were all shining brightly, and a small northwest wind was starting to blow all across the Plains, from the Crow far away in the west to the Mississippi on the east. It would be twenty below zero in the morning.

Ron was deep in the cave now, with the wind whirling around the entrance, blowing snow inside for about ten feet every once in a while. He was not in a mood to deal with it right now. He had never seen a winter like this with a high number of days below zero and a feet of snow piled everywhere. His daily chores were taking longer each day because of the deep snow and drifts everywhere. Just finding, cutting, and carrying firewood into the cave all took way longer than normal. Ron was wishing spring would hurry up and get here. Shadow thought it was nice as long as the dry grass held out. It would not be fun digging in the deep snow now for dead grass and then eating it.

The next few days were very windy, with snow coming down like it would never end. It was very deep in most places and almost impossible to ride very far before your horse was worn out. It was best to stay put for now, and everyone in the west did just that.

The Crow had spent seven days inside their tepees when the wind slowed way down, and the snow stopped. They needed to get upside and do something, and this morning, they sent a hunting party out to look for deer, elk, or buffalo. Another party looked for firewood, and the rest of the camp started packing snow down, building big fires, and making hanging racks for the meat to cure on as well as to stay high and away from the bears.

Everything was ready when the first group came in with two deer to butcher. The Crow were talking fast and enjoying their work, knowing that later they would have a feast of deer soup. Nothing would be wasted from this animal or any other one that gave its life for them. Tomorrow would be more work with the hides and bones, making blankets, coats, spoons, arrowheads, and needles. Just then, another group came in with an elk. The work would be for many days to help cure the meat, work the hides, and store all of it away where the animals of the wild couldn't come and destroy it.

Six hundred miles to the west of the Crow, the people of the wagon train were doing the same. Ole and his group had been out hunting too and had a great deal of success. They had brought in three elk and four big fat buck deer. The women had been rendering lard, the children helping with the making of jerky, and the men cutting the big pieces into smaller roasts and things like that for preserving in salt. *Soon,* Pete thought, *we will be looking for more salt too.* The meat cellar would be full tonight when they had finished whole process. That would be good since they had been having so much snow lately. *Plenty of food is never bad.*

Ron was back in the cave, polishing his fine revolvers and rubbing them down again and again. Then he applied a thin layer of some fine, three-in-one oil all over it except on the grips. He wanted them not slippery. Then he did the same to his big rifles and the rest of his weapons. He took off his holster and rubbed mink oil into it until it was as soft as a baby's bottom. Now he was ready for whoever was brave enough to come looking for him.

Ron's packhorse was doing fine with them not traveling now. As a matter of fact, he was getting a little overweight. He was checking him out while he was oiling her cargo saddles and harnesses. He also polished his riding saddle and gun scabbards. *Everything is in top shape,* he thought as he leaned back against the cave wall. He was wondering who the first to come looking for him would be. That thought sent a chill up his spine. He had better watch his back. *Especially the closer it gets toward spring.*

"Eyes behind your head in everything you do from now on," he told himself in a low whisper.

A bunch of the men were sitting outside by the fire at the center of the wagon train when Ole walked up, sat down, and started to clean his rifle. They were talking about all the things that needed to be decided on before they left this campsite, if they were even leaving now. A few of the people wanted to stay here and enjoy this little valley with its beauty, and others wanted to move on. Ole was kind of fond of this little town that they had built. He thought that it was not the right time to decide on anything because it was late in the day, but some of it needed to be decided on soon. And he was right.

Later that evening, they had talked themselves out, and all of them decided to figure the whole mess out early someday, not at night, when everyone was tired. Soon they were all looking for their wagon and were turning in for the night.

All across the land, from the east to the west, everyone had turned in for the night. Even Mr. Winter was not out tonight as it was a lot warmer than normal as of late. It was close to twenty degrees warmer than normal tonight. Spring would be sticking its head around the corner and into their lives soon, for it was late March now. Soon spring would be galloping in like a big stallion herding his females away from another.

It was a beautiful spring morning today as the sun was starting its way into the sky above the frozen earth. It was fairly warm; the wind was gone, and it felt warmer than it really was. In some protected areas where the sun was shining brightly on an object like a rock, it was melting the snow all around. Here and there, some grass was showing up through the snow, which was disappearing all around it. Soon spring would be here in full force.

The birds were singing at the edge of the big meadow near the cave that Ron was using as his winter home. They had been singing all morning because of its beauty, the warm air, and the absence of a strong wind.

At the opposite side, a herd of white-tailed deer emerged from the wooded area surrounding the meadow. There were ten females and one large buck in the group. The buck was the strongest of all the bucks from last year. He had won the honor of being herd bull now after winning. This year, all the fawns would be his offspring, and he was proud of that fact. He ran around the females, blowing his horn and showing his stout form to all the females and any male caught looking from the side. He was the king. But today he was just walking out of the woods, looking for dry grass sticking up and out of the remaining snow. They were hungry after the long winter with the deep snow. Pawing for grass all winter was a lot of work. *Better than starving to death,* he thought.

The snow was melting faster now and was causing little gullies of water to start running down the hill. Then the little gullies would run into another, and the two of them would form a bigger gully that would run downhill until it found another one, and soon it would be a fairly large stream. And then toward the bottom of the mountain, the streams would turn into creeks and creeks into rivers. In some areas, the river would become very large and out of control, flooding thousands of acres up to ten feet deep. This was always a fear for the frontiersmen because most camps or settlements were near water. But being too close or in the wrong spot, one could be flooded out every year.

The deer had spotted several bands of coyotes and wolves today while they were grazing. The wolves always stayed at the edge of the woods in the cover of the underbrush, looking for a way to get close to the deer and try for a kill. However, today the deer were on high alert, and they stayed on the other side of the meadow from anything that looked or smelled like danger. If something that they didn't know moved, they moved quickly to a new location. Soon they would be giving birth to the new fawns, so eating all day long was required to build up the body reserves for the youngsters.

Tonight as the sun settled in, all the people of the Plains were thinking about springtime and the variety of smells that filled the air—fresh air, rain, wild flowers, growing plants, and many others that your mind could not even name. They were followed by a beauty that would be hard to believe as the leaves and flowers would start to explode all around them.

Anna was lying next to Pete as he slept, and she was thinking about the smells in the air and all this springtime stuff when she thought, *How could you not believe in God when you get to see this and smell it too?* She lay there for a long time, thinking about this topic and listening to the stream outside the camp sing as it let the water go down the river. It was so comforting to her to know that God controlled all of it, and at the same time, he made it pretty and smell good. She was thinking about how God made all of creation and made it work to perfection when she finally fell asleep.

This spring came in fast and furious. It went from minus twenty degrees to temperatures in the sixties in just a couple of days. The snow all melted in the first week, and then all the greenery started to add leaves, stems, or roots. It was turning very green fast during this second week of beautiful weather. Some of the mountain streams were so big that they had washed a new path across the land and hastened the rush to the bottom, where it made the creeks go over the banks and wash out more land. That had continued all the way down the mountainside until it reached the rivers, and then they overflowed. Two weeks ago, there had been water all over the valleys below, but now it had settled into the soil pretty well.

Oh-y-Yee and her friends sure noticed the difference in the weather. It was so much warmer that they felt hot most of the time now; instead of trying to find a windbreak to stay away from the cold wind, now they wanted a cooler wind. She noticed her coat was letting go of its grip on her hide now. Once in a while when she bumped a tree or something like that, a clump of hair would fall out and float to the ground. *That just means that summer is nearby,* she thought. Oh-y-Yee remembered from the former years that when your hair wanted to fly, soon it would be hot outside in the barren areas.

All her friends had been running around the meadow every day now, and so had she. It was too nice in the meadow to sit around doing nothing; plus, she wanted to see where the best grass was starting to grow so she would know where to graze. Oh-y-Yee already knew where the best grass was this year, and she was hoarding it. After running and working up a sweat, she and the others would roll around in the dust, working off the dead and dying hair. Then they would run again for a half hour or so and then again until they were real tired. Then they would do the final roll, scratch, and kick in the dust to dry them off so they would not catch a cold or have that long winter hair into the summer. They would all be bright and shiny like a brand-new nickel.

It was a beautiful day, and Oh-y-Yee was enjoying every breath of it out here in the meadow just over the knoll from the rest of the herd. She was twisting the grass off the stem with her powerful lips and long front teeth. She was lost in her thoughts when she realized she was not alone. Oh-y-Yee stopped reaching for grass, looked up, and saw that ugly black mare standing there looking like she owned the place. She was four and a half years old, quite big, and wide in the chest.

Oh-y-Yee was not scared at all and was ready to defend her position in the herd as the alpha female. She started trotting toward the black bitch with her ears pinned back against her head and her front feet ready for a kickboxing match that would not last long, if she had her way. It was important for Oh-y-Yee to look superfast and powerful so that all the other females in the herd would respect her even more after the challenge.

She ran into the black mare, kicking like a wild woman, and then reached out and bit her high up on the neck, trying to show her superior strength and power along with the alpha position. Suddenly, she turned and threw a high hard kick directly into the face of the black horse, almost knocking her out. That was all that was needed to make her turn and run, with Oh-y-Yee running and biting her rump. The entire herd watched as Oh-y-Yee cleaned her clock and then returned to eating grass as if nothing had happened. *I am the alpha, and they had better notice,* she thought as she continued to eat the choice long grass. No one else would challenge her this year, and that was a fact. No one did.

Chapter 12

Ron was high up in the mountains today, looking for a small deer or a few rabbits for tonight's meal. But he was also scouting to see if anyone had been up this high, looking for him. So far, he had not seen any hoofprints that belonged to a horse with shoes on it or one that was carrying a load. He was always worried about running into someone out here in the wilderness who would see his clothes and gear. They would not have to ask what he did for a living, but they would ask why he was out here in the Wild West alone.

You see, Ron was a gunfighter, and he had to leave his last town in a hurry and did not have time to get a change of clothing. It was about ten o'clock at night when the gunfight started, and five minutes later, it was over. Three good old cowboys were lying on the floor dead, bullet holes through their foreheads. They had been playing cards with the slick gentlemen who rode in all fancied up that afternoon. Ron had cheated them, and they caught him. They were mad when Tony drew his gun, and they all ended up on the floor dead without even knowing what had happened.

Ron had barely escaped town that night and had to ride hard for several days before the sheriff gave up and went back to town. Shadow had earned his respect that night and for the next few days as well. But Ron had on what he called his fancy pants, his show boots, his fancy double Colts, his holster, and his buckskin shirt with the big, wide leather cowboy hat that had been specially made for him. No one out in this wood looked anywhere close to him. They were working people. He wasn't.

Seven hundred miles east of here, two bounty hunters were getting ready to start looking for Ron and Shadow. Both were important to know because Shadow wore two hot brands on his rump, one on each side. He wore a pony express brand on his right side, which was a WF&C for Wells Fargo & Company, and on his left side a brand that was very familiar to Ron, the R-W. It was his father's brand, and it was well known in the eastern part of the Kansas Flint Hills, where the R-W ranch was located. It was one of the biggest and best ranches in all Kansas, with thousands of acres of wonderful grass. Ron's dad and three brothers ran the ranch today. Ron was invited to be a part of it, but he always thought cows were a waste of time.

He had more fun growing up in the little woods next to the barn, where he was always the sheriff who had to arrest the bad guys. He became a wiz at firing a gun and hitting targets. Riding horses was natural for him.

Now he had made a big mistake and was running from the law himself. More than once, he had caught himself wishing he could back up and do it all over the right way. But that was not going to happen, so he was running from the law and would be for the rest of his life. He was worried about the double brand on Shadow, but he couldn't just leave him somewhere like he was just another horse. Besides, if he left him, someone would notice. Then they would know they were close to him. *At least now they are guessing about my whereabouts,* he thought.

Ron was now headed back toward the cave with several rabbits to make stew. He had found some greens that would work well with his catch. Tomorrow would be another day, and hopefully, he could scout some more around the top of this mountain to see if anyone was looking for him. He had found several Indian trails today that were very well hidden along the edge of the forest. The trails went straight through several big growths of wild berries and thickets of cedar trees. Ron was thinking about the trail and wondering how many miles a guy could travel here unnoticed.

Now he had entered a clearing where the grass was getting tall and blowing in the wind. *It is peaceful and beautiful,* he thought. Shadow had picked up the pace because he had realized they were heading toward the cave, and that meant he would be allowed to eat grass, roll in the dirt, and rest until tomorrow. Shadow would sleep well tonight, but Ron wondered if he would. Most of the time when he had thought about the gunfight, he did not sleep well nor for a very long period. They traveled for about three hours through some very rough country that was steep and covered with small bushes and brush before reaching the entrance of the cave. They were hungry and tired.

Ole was up early this morning, and he didn't know why. He was walking around the little village, thinking about the big gun blast they had heard a couple of months ago when they were hunting south of here. Who was it? Why were they way up there at that time of the year? He was thinking, *When the weather gets nicer and warmer, I may take a couple of the guys up there and do some scouting around to see if there is any sign of life.*

Ole started the big circle firepit at the center of the camp now and was putting the coffeepot over the fire when Pete and Al showed up. They started talking about all the improvements they had made, and now they were wondering if that would make it even harder for some of them to leave it behind and head west. They discussed it awhile, and then the subject changed to the Crow. Pete brought it up to the other two and said they had better be watching from now on because the Crow would only fight in the summer, and they had seen all kinds of signs of the Crow around here last fall. Big Al said that before he joined the train last fall, he had run into the Crow, and they were looking for a wagon train group that had violated the burial grounds by driving straight through it while knocking down several burial platforms.

Pete and Ole had a long, pale, and sober look on their faces when Big Al turned to look at them. "It was you!" Al shouted. Both Ole and Pete nodded and then started to explain what had happened. Pete said they were clear into the middle of it before they realized it was a burial ground. They tried to get the wagons and cattle through it without damage, but that was not possible. They had knocked some of the stands over, and the wagon wheels had made deep ruts through others. After that day, they had seen Crow braves up in the mountains on the north side several times a week, and then they were gone.

Silence was there for a couple of minutes before Big Al cleared his throat and said, "Well, I guess we had better start digging in here for the next few months, building a wall around camp, making sure we have water into the camp and plenty of food around. We will need to start having sentries day and night and sending more men out when hunting. Many things will need to be done soon. This is the worst thing that can happen to the Crow, and they will all die before you will be free from their evil desires for you and your families. Nothing will stop them."

Wow! It was really quiet now, and others had joined the circle around the roaring fire. Some wanted to leave as soon as possible. Others wanted to build a big fortress here, and some even wanted to turn back eastward until they reached Iowa. There was plenty of discussion to last more than just today. They had work to do today, and all of them decided that tomorrow afternoon they would meet again to figure out a plan of action.

The rest of the day, the people from the train were looking over their shoulders and wondered what they should do—stay or head west fast. Anna was the only one in the group who stood up and suggested that they talk with the Crow and let them know they were sorry for what they had done. "If the Crow found out that we didn't know it was a burial ground, maybe they would show mercy," she said. "And that may help soothe it over."

Big Al jumped to his feet and shouted, "The only thing the Crow want now is your scalp hanging from their lodgepole! Nothing else!"

It was a very warm spring day in this meadow in the center of western Montana where the Crow had moved to in the early fall of last year. Hie sun was high in the sky, and it seemed brighter than normal. There was a slight breeze that moved the pretty yellow flowers back and forth on the wild daisy plants, which made it look like the blades of green grass went the opposite direction. There was no sound anywhere in the meadow except the sound of the slight breeze moving through the grass.

Oh-y-Yee was lying halfway up on the side of a little hill in the center of the meadow. She was flat out and sleeping. She started dreaming about her birth and family. Her mother was licking her all over, trying to dry her off shortly after birth, when Oh-y-Yee opened one eye and then the other to look at her mom for the first time. She remembered that her mother's color was a deep dark gray that was almost black with a tight coat that seemed to shine in the sunlight. Her mane and tail were black as were her hooves. Her mother was also very tall and strong with heavy hindquarters full of muscles. She was almost as tall, strong, and good looking as Oh-y-Yee.

After a couple of months, Oh-y-Yee was running through the meadow where she was born when she met her dad for the first time. He was a very strong, tall, and long stallion that definitely could be the alpha male in a band of wild horses for a long time. He had a very light gray color with dapples in it that looked like snowflakes. His mane and tail were also light colored, more of a blue hue to the gray than what was normal. He had solid black hooves with very dark-colored eyes. There was no doubt he was the stallion of the herd. When he moved through the herd, it was like he was prancing along with ease in a stately manner. *He is very impressive,* she thought as he ran away with his tail high in the air above his back. She wanted to grow up and be just as impressive.

Oh-y-Yee ran hard every day for her first two years, trying to build her muscles and shape. Soon she had found out she was the biggest female in the herd with heavy muscles and athletic skills that were above average. Hers were way above average.

Not long after that, the Crow had surprised the herd early one morning, and Oh-y-Yee had been captured and taken away from them. She had not seen her parents since then and was wondering if they were still alive or long gone. *They should be alive,* she thought, *maybe around twelve years of age.* That happened in southern Utah in a canyon that led to a nice meadow after going through some monument rocks that pointed high into the sky in many colors. Oh-y-Yee wondered if she had any sisters or brothers and, if so, how many.

Suddenly, she was startled by a loud noise and was wide awake, and her dream was over. It was what seemed to be every horse in the herd, running by her at once with feet and tails in the air. Oh-y-Yee joined in with the herd, running wildly around the meadow and then slowing down to a walk and finally stopping. Now the entire herd was slowly grazing along the edge of the meadow, with just a couple of newborn colts running from one horse to another throughout the afternoon. Soon there would be many new colts, and she wondered if she would ever become a mother. She would have to find the stallion, and she hoped he was handsome.

The next morning, the wagon train's people could hardly think while doing their morning chores. This afternoon, they would discuss their future on whether to journey on westward when spring came or to stay here and build a town. They were all very busy going back and forth throughout camp doing their chores.

The day was very nice, with the temperature around sixty-five degrees and a slight breeze and the smell of spring in the air. Some of the men were coming into camp now with fresh meat, mostly deer and elk. Others were bringing in more firewood while the rest of them had prepared the noon meal and set up chunks of firewood as chairs for the meeting. Some of them were eating and getting ready for the debate.

Pete stood up and asked if Lars would open with a Bible reading and prayer, which he gladly did. Then Pete had Big Al give an eye-opening speech about the Crow and their beliefs on honoring the dead and their resting places. Then came the part about how they dealt with trespassers. The women and children were scared by it, and some of them started crying.

Then Thomas told everyone the plus and minus of staying or moving on. He opened it up for questions from the group. The first question was for Big Al from Alfred; he asked if this stream ran year round and if it had been doing that for years. Al nodded and said that he had never seen it dry before. Then came the question about the land around here. Was it good farmland? Was it great for corn or just grasses? Would they have to irrigate it? How far was it to a major market for the goods they would produce? The meeting went on and on until they had covered everything you could think of and then some.

Someone asked, "If we packed up and left, when would we go, and how long would it take to get to our new home in California?" Pete thought about it for a moment and then said it would take the rest of the year to get to California if they were lucky and if the snow didn't hit the Sierra mountains early. They may be fighting the Crow all the way to California, and that would make time fly away without going anywhere, just pinned down, hoping they could get the upper hand and start moving again.

After eight hours of debating, they decided to stay here, build a fortress, and stay another year. If they survived, they could move on the following year. If not, they would just die right here at home. Pete said they could always stay here and build this one-horse town into a big city too.

The meeting had gone well, but Pete was very tired when he crawled into bed beside Anna. She was awake, and they spoke for about an hour. They were glad they were going to stay until next year, but they would have to be ready for the Crow. That was rule 1 in being alive when next year came around.

The next morning came very fast, and everyone was hustling this and that way, seeming to know just what had to be done and when. Some were bringing in new firewood, others were feeding the horses, and some were already far out into the forest cutting trees down, trimming them, and getting them ready for the long drag into town. Things were getting done at a record pace around the train today. Pete was impressed with the way Ole could rally the people and get them excited about making things go smooth and fast without mistakes or foolish injuries. He was a natural in motivating the people.

Fred and his group were digging big holes along the south edge of the compound to put the big logs into. They would be standing on end with the top sharpened and pointing toward the sky so the Crow would have a big surprise when trying to climb over them. Ole was laughing when he thought about the Crow trying to crawl over the top with all its sharp points sticking them right in the privates while everyone in camp was shooting at them. Ole went to Fred and told him why he had been laughing, and they both began to laugh harder as they thought more about it. Pete walked up and said he wanted barbed wire strung across the top foot and a half of the wall, and Ole and Fred laughed so hard that they gathered a crowd to see what was going on. Ole said he could just picture a Crow hanging from the top pointed end with a hole through his privates, caught up in barbed wire, and bullets flying all over the place. It felt good to get something done.

Chapter 13

Over in central Montana, the Crow were also out and about. The hunting party was out looking for some fresh buffalo to shoot and butcher. Others were out in the meadows playing war games, and some were working with the horses. Some of the older braves were making spear and arrowheads while others made the shaft for each head made. A few older women had also arrived and were sewing buckskin and shaping it into quivers, sheaths, and fancy shirts to be used only on the first raid of the year. It was the holy "dreaded hand" shirt with a big black circle with a white hand in the center.

Some of the younger boys were hauling in firewood as fast as they could, trying to build up muscles so that they would be worthy of being a brave this year. It was an honor to be considered, let alone be selected, but every young boy in the camp wanted to be selected when he was young so that he could prove himself worthy in front of his parents and grandparents. All of them wanted to be the chief someday.

The young girls were sewing and singing songs while working. They were old tribal songs that had been passed down for hundreds of years. One of the songs was about the Great Spirit, who only did the right things and was superclean and the Father of all. All the members of the tribe liked this song because it put them at ease just knowing about him and his umnatchable power. This song started many others singing songs about the Great Spirit until late into the night.

The Crow horses in the meadow were running back and forth, racing one another in pretend games and wars. The little colts were just starting to be born, with the oldest being three weeks old. They were running around the older horses, kicking up their heels, and racing back and forth with never-ending energy. Soon the older horses slowed down and grazed in the meadow, wondering what the other horses that had left this morning were now doing. Most likely, they were hunting or watching the skinning of the buffalo while being loaded with meat. Little did they know what was about to happen next.

There was a cloud of dust as Oh-y-Yee and Awanatu crashed into the earth thirty feet below the trail on the mountainside above. He was under her at the base of the cliff, with the air knocked out of him. She also had the air knocked out of her lungs, and both of them were struggling to breathe. Oh-y-Yee had slid off him and was setting off to the side, dazed. Awanatu was out cold and was just struggling to keep the air coming into his lungs. He had blood coming from his ears and mouth with teeth missing. He must have broken bones in the fall, but no one could tell until he came back to the living.

A few minutes later, the braves of the Crow had found a way around the cliff and down to the crash site. They were excited and wondering what to do first. Some of them made a bed out of branches and pine boughs while others helped move him on top of them. They were holding horseradish roots under his nose, hoping to bring him back to normal. He was groaning now and having trouble breathing. The Crow decided to haul him back to camp on a stretcher made from two logs tied over a horse's rump with a blanket in between. They could see that he was hurt badly, with one arm broken and maybe also one leg. He was in bad shape.

Oh-y-Yee was now standing next to where they landed, dazed, confused, and hurting. She had a thumping feeling in her head that felt like a freight train going through at eighty miles per hour when it derailed on loose gravel. Her legs were sore, and one ankle felt broken. One hour passed before Oh-y-Yee could remember bits and pieces of what had happened. Another hour passed, and she was getting better at remembering the facts of the afternoon.

She remembered the high speed she had attained just before rounding the corner and seeing the tree planted in the center of the trail. She hit it at full gallop, and the power in the branches swung her off the trail and over the cliff. That was the last thing she remembered until now. The landing had knocked the wind out of her and had bruised her left side deep into the muscles. Oh-y-Yee was very sore and stiff, with minor cuts all over her left side. She could not put any weight on her left ankle either.

Oh-y-Yee was feeling bad for Awanatu after she came to and remembered what had happened, even though she had wanted to hurt him before. This was an accident, and she wanted to punish him directly but not this way. He was hurt, and she could see it was bad, even for him.

All the Crow braves were helping get Awanatu into the hammock behind one of the horses with the least amount of pain possible. He was screaming like a young boy, with blood running from his mouth and ears. He seemed to be in another world full of pain when one of the older braves shoved some kind of weed into his mouth and made him chew it until he could swallow it. Soon he was out of pain and snoring like a fat hog. He wouldn't feel a thing on the way back to camp.

A couple of braves had carved some braces out of cottonwood that fit Oh-y-Yee's ankle and foreleg perfectly. Now they laced it up tightly and tied it in place. It made a big difference, and she felt better instantly. *It will be many moons before everyone is healed front this accident,* thought Oh-y-Yee as she was limping back toward camp. She did not know it at the time, but she was right; it would take many moons.

Awanatu was starting to wake up as the sun was setting in the west with a dark red color. He wasn't sure if it was his injuries or if the sun was actually red in color. The back of his head felt like thirty horses had run over him with each hoof kicking it while stepping down hard on it. He was dizzy, his legs could not hold his weight up at all, and he was in no way strong enough to stay upright anyway. Soon he quit struggling and fell asleep on the big buffalo robe in the center of the tepee.

It had been hard getting him back here to the campsite. Trees had caught the pole cart as they were going through the woods, and then they had to be removed or the sled dragged backward for a bit and then try it again. He was in a lot of pain and had many injuries that needed time to heal, like all the broken ribs and his leg. His mouth was very swollen with several teeth missing and maybe a broken jaw. *Awanatu would be lucky to live another year,* thought Oh-y-Yee. The war party would not be going after the settlers this year after all.

The Crow were all now helping with the injuries to the braves and their horses. The old medicine man was dancing and offering up prayers for them while the squaws were making root and beef soups that had been known to heal internal injuries for centuries. Some of the braves and old men were doctoring the horses while others did the normal chores around the campsite.

Back at the settlers' camp along the creek, everyone was working very hard, trying to get the job done on time. Pete, Big Al, and Ole had assigned jobs to everyone. This was very important to their survival as they told the group. They had to be ready to defend the campsite against the Crow, who were surely coming.

Chapter 14

Awanatu was sleeping hard, with dreams of the Great Spirit coming down to the earth to take him away. He was going into shock and coming out of it seconds later. It was touch and go for him. His dreams were wild, with him being the great chief who would bring all the Indians of the Plains together. In the next one, he would be fighting a big black bear, and so on it went well into the night. Each dream was different with various outcomes. Sometimes he was hurt badly, and in the next, he was the hero. The herbal tea was making his mind go crazy for many hours in a row before, exhausted, he fell into deep sleep.

Each day was getting warmer now with the sweet smell of spring being in the air. Pete sat down on a stump near his wagon when Anna came out and sat next to him. She reached out, grabbed his hand, and gave him a big kiss along with "I love you." Pete replied that he also loved her.

They just sat there for a while without talking, just smelling the freshness of springtime and looking around, when Anna asked him what he was thinking about. Pete started out by saying that he was impressed with the smells in the air and the beauty all around them and that it must be a gift from God. He also said that he knew their son was up there now with God, and he understood why. Anna asked him why and he said God wanted them out West but knew they would never go away from Iowa if they had children to share with their parents. God also knew that they would leave Iowa because of the bad memories that had been there. "For some reason, God wants us out West," Pete said.

Now Anna said, "Maybe we won't make it after wandering into the Crow cemetery."

"Nah," said Pete, "God is stronger than they are."

The work around the campsite was continuing each and every day, and today was no exception. Logs were being dragged into camp, logs being sawed into boards, and boards becoming buildings. Women were cooking stew in the big copper pots all day long as workers came in shifts to eat. Others were working in the garden or digging the trench from the creek to the center of town, where more men were digging a deep hole in the ground to store water. This trench would be lined with boards on all four sides and then covered with dirt so the Crow would not know the settlers had water. *That is pretty sharp,* thought Ole. He also smelled the scent of spring in the air.

Big Al wandered over to Pete and Anna and said, "I don't think it will snow anymore this year, and soon the grass will be a foot high out here on the meadow, and that is when we will have to watch out for the Crow." Anna thought that comment ruined a wonderful time she was having with Pete, so she picked herself up, gave Pete a kiss, and said goodbye to Al.

Al asked Pete if he had said something wrong, and Pete said "No, she is leaving anyway."

In the big, tall pine tree sat the old eagle on the side of the nest. His young female friend was sitting in the center like a queen. She had three eggs underneath her chest, and she could hear and smell the babies inside. She was so excited about this upcoming event that she was forgetting to go hunting. But that didn't seem to matter in the least because her old friend seemed to have a new level of energy she hadn't seen before. He was alert and bright eyed. He was also a great provider of food.

The old eagle sat on the edge of the nest thinking about the beautiful smell of spring in the air. It was also refreshing to behold. He also heard and could smell the babies in the eggs beneath his young friend, and it made him proud. It made him feel twenty years younger. Hunting was easy now as all the mice were hungry after a long winter underground. They were fat and plump.

Ron was way up in the high country now, sitting outside his cave's entrance, smelling the fresh air of spring. The trees were starting to bud out, the flowers were ready to blossom, the snow was melting, and water was running faster down the mountainside, only to find a river that was suddenly twice as big as before. The animals were out looking for something to eat or a place to give birth to the next generation. But all of them could smell that spring was here and knew what to do next because God had put that in their mind when he made them. Even Ron believed that God had done all this in the blink of an eye.

A week passed by, and the Crow thought it was a month. Many of the young men were still injured so bad that they couldn't get out of their hammocks. The women were feeding them, washing them, changing their buckskins for them, and putting ointment on their wounds.

Oh-y-Yee was wondering how Awanatu was doing or if he was even alive. She had not seen him in over two weeks now, nor had she seen many of his friends. The grass was growing, and she was devouring all that she could find each day. Running around the meadow was also a daily thing she did without missing. If her rider couldn't be at full speed and power this year, she was. The young stallion was long forgotten now when the real problem came along. Oh-y-Yee wanted Awanatu to survive and become strong again so that she could have her turn with him out in the High Desert somewhere. She was working hard for that day.

Awanatu was sleeping better now but still had bad dreams almost every night. Last night, he was dreaming wildly. He was the highest-ranking brave in the Crow nation and had earned the name Wild Cat. He was the most feared of all and was ruthless in his manners. He would kill and scalp or scalp and kill; it didn't seem to matter. His enemies trembled with fear when they saw him coming toward them. In one battle, he killed eighteen warriors alone in one afternoon. At the dance that night, they made him the chief of all Crow. He woke up and found out that it was only a dream, which made him very angry. He was so mad that he tried getting out of his hammock and ended up falling out of it. They put him back into it and made him drink more herb tea, and soon he was sleeping hard. Nothing was going to bother him now.

Nightfall came, and the stars were out bright, with a full moon to dance around. Everyone and everything knew that God had made it all. Even the little frozen crystals around the edge of the pond knew that God had created them. It all seemed so peaceful and beautiful that one could just look at its beauty forever without being bored with it.

The next morning, the Crow were up early, starting the day's work, when a scream came from one of the tepees. Everyone was dashing from tepee to tepee to see what had happened when another scream came from the north end of the encampment. All the braves went running to the north with their weapons in hand and the rest of the villagers following. Upon arriving, they found Awanatu wildly swinging his tomahawk at anyone who would get close while singing a famous war chant about killing the enemy and lifting his scalp. The Crow braves had surrounded him but couldn't get close without getting hurt by the wild swings.

After a few minutes, he dropped his guard for a few seconds, and then several warriors jumped him from behind and made him surrender. Back to his tepee they went. After some more herbal tea, he was sound asleep. Now the morning was normal again, and everyone was doing their part in their chores and talking about Awanatu and how crazy he had been lately.

Some of the older braves had left camp to seek deer or buffalo. It was a lot better this time of the year to hunt for large game as they left a deeper imprint of their hooves in the ground and therefore were easier to track. The men were excited to be outside and go hunting instead of working inside the tepees. The smell of spring was in the air stronger than ever today after the small shower that came through last night. Everything was fresh again.

The women of the camp were cleaning their tepees, making food, or sewing new buckskins for their family members. It seemed like they were always busy with something.

Hie children were playing in the nearby meadow along the creek. They had surprise attacks on pretend soldiers and settlers as well as on their pretend buffalo herd. They played hard, running all through the valley's meadow, creek, and hillside. They would be laughing one minute and then screaming to the top of their lungs the next.

One old man named Slippery Fish was watching them and smiling as he thought back to his childhood. He was many moons old now with long white hair mixed with wrinkled gray skin. His eyesight was poor, but the smell in the air and the sounds of the children brought back many fond memories of his childhood. Slippery Fish had lost his wife a few moons ago, and his life was changed forever from that moment on. He knew he would be visiting the Great Spirit soon, and he was preparing for that day. Somehow he was at total ease in the thought of seeing God and being with him. The smell of spring was in the air as Slippery Fish hung his head and crossed over the vast prairie to meet God.

The news spread throughout the camp almost instantly about Slippery Fish. Everyone was now preparing for the meal and the dancing until the wee hours of the morning while singing old Crow songs about being delivered to the great God who made all the earth and continued to make it run smoothly.

The next morning, the Crow started a long march to one of the burial grounds with the lifeless body of Slippery Fish. He would be wrapped in his finest buffalo robes and put high on the burial stand with some of his favorite weapons to protect him on his journey to the Great Spirit. They also included food for him and his horse, which would be buried below him but under his deck. The Crow sang more songs of bravery and the Great Spirit before putting him away forever.

The last thing they did was to hang his shield, bow, and arrows and all scalps taken during their wars to his lodgepoles. He had been a very brave warrior all his life, but more importantly, he was a good father figure and an honest man. It was clear that the people loved him as they were reluctant to leave the sacred burial grounds to go back to the campsite.

The old eagle had been flying around the western part of his hunting site when he had spotted the Crow at the burial grounds. He had flown lower than normal to see who had died when the Crow spotted him. They cried out loud with songs and wailings about the Great Spirit coming down to swoop Slippery Fish away in the form of the great eagle. It was a sign that he had been lifted to the great place in the sky to enjoy happy hunting forever.

Ron had been riding west of his encampment for four days when he spotted the Crow heading toward the sacred burial grounds, and he was wondering who had died and how. He dismounted and watched from behind some big gooseberry bushes until they had all went by. *It is someone important to the Crow,* Ron thought after they had passed by with so many in the group. He wondered how and who.

The settlers were wrapping it up for the day with the finishing details of their chores. Some of the women were fixing the evening meal, and others were rounding up the children, making sure they had washed their hands. The smell of springtime was still in the air, and it was now mixed with the smell of a great beef stew cooking in big pots inside the circle of wagons. All was good.

Chapter 15

Ole, Pete, Big Al, and some of the men were sitting off to the side, talking about the future. They were discussing the plans for the fortress surrounding the camp and which buildings would need to be built next. They loved the big building in the center of the camp, which provided a place for everyone to have meals, meetings, weddings, and church services. The root cellar was also great to preserve their food throughout the winter, and now with the addition of the underground water tank, they wondered what should be next. Big Al was sure that they needed to continue the tall log wall so that it surrounded the entire camp. It would be easy to defend compared with a makeshift assortment of logs pulled into a pile. The discussion went on until it was time to eat, and it would continue later.

This new and refreshing smell of springtime is intoxicating to one's mind, thought Pete as he sat along the south side of the group, eating his meal. It was nice to see the people show renewed energy. Things would go faster now and smoother too.

It was near sunset, and all the animals of the prairie were out hunting or grazing. They too enjoyed the smell of spring that the Great Spirit sent to them, telling them that the winter was over and that the grass was growing again. A small herd of deer were grazing not far from the camp; up on the mountainside, a bear was digging through a rotting log, looking for grubs. In a faraway place, the howl of a group of wolves was heard. They were hunting and telling one another where to go or where to be to make the kill.

Several weeks passed by in no time flat. The changes in nature were made each day around them by God, and they hardly noticed it. But change it had.

The grass in the meadow was now nearly knee high, with many spots of wild flowers growing. A little gust of wind would come by every once in a while, making it look like a lake of water with flowers floating in it. It was beautiful, and the smell had changed from that strong springtime aroma to that of flowers. The buds on the branches of the trees had also changed to leaves with the color of green in many different shades. From a dark blue green to a light lime green, the colors were as if they had picked them out themselves. They were just beautiful from every angle and even better when the wind was blowing. The bees and the birds were busy finding food or building their new homes for the summer. The bees had located all the big flowers and were drinking nectar like a drunk in a saloon. The birds were catching insects and worms and taking them back to their mates in the nest. Their mates were busy sitting on eggs and waiting for the next generation to hatch. The deer, antelope, and moose were out in the meadow as well, eating their fill of nice green grass. In some parts, the buffalo were grazing too. Baby calves were starting to arrive. When they were first born, they would run and jump, getting their legs and feet to work in case they had to run for their lives soon after birth. The ground squirrels, gophers, wolverines, and mice were all remodeling or building new homes. The thawed-out ground was much easier to dig in than the hard-packed ground from last fall.

Oh-y-Yee was lying on a sidehill, sunning herself in the warm spring sunshine, thinking about how thankful she should be for not getting hurt worse than she did in the fall off the path that injured Awanatu so badly. She only felt a little pain in her ankle now and then. It was almost completely healed. *The Great Spirit is with me that day,* she thought as she continued to lie in the sunshine. Later, she would do her daily run around the pasture, kicking up her heels in defiance. She would someday prove that she was the queen of all. Until that day came, she was going to work hard and harder.

The Crow were all outside today unless they were injured badly. The men had brought in a freshly killed deer and had skinned it; they now were tanning the hide while the women were cutting the meat and drying it until it was jerky. Others were taking the scraps and putting them into a big pot to make fresh stew for tonight. Tonight there would be dancing and a feast because it was the first hunt of spring, which made it special.

Some of the braves were playing war games on foot and shooting arrows into lifelike statues of white men. They were having fun, and they won each battle and collected many scalps. Then they started telling stories about previous real wars, and each time, they were the hero and did better than the time before. The old men nearby laughed at them, thinking that they had once sounded just like them, as they shook their heads.

Awanatu wanted to be outside doing something besides just lying around the tepee. He was healing some now, but it had been long and slow. He was working a little every day by making arrowheads, knife handles, and spear poles. He was ready for something else to do that was exciting and fun, like chasing the palefaces and making them pay for their sins.

That night, Awanatu fell fast asleep and went straight into a long and wild dream where he was chasing the white eyes that had violated the holy grounds. He would kill some with his spear, some with his knife, and others with his big bare hands. In the end, all the whites were killed and their scalps taken. Suddenly, he was wide awake with his eyes wide open, looking for the white eyes. When he came to, he realized that he had been dreaming the dream of his life. He was angry now, thinking that the palefaces had escaped again, and he would have to work harder than ever before to be ready for them in real life.

In the past two weeks, he had improved rapidly so that now he could walk around the campsite slowly and carefully. He was healing on the inside more than he knew. It would be at least a year before he would ride again, but he didn't know that, nor would he want to. Some of the other braves were healing much faster than he was, and that was also annoying him.

Out in the pasture, Oh-y-Yee was enjoying her time off from the everyday chore of riding into the woods and meadows as fast as she could run and then having Awanatu pull the reins back as hard as he could while trying to stop on a dime. Each time he did that, she was totally pissed. It made no sense to her. *But it did keep me in shape,* she thought. Now she was getting heavier each day, and that also worried her. Then she wandered back into the meadow to graze.

Far off to the east about seven hundred miles sat Ron next to a roaring fire while roasting a pheasant he had caught in a snare in the high meadow to the east side of his cave. He was thinking how life had changed for him in the last few months. Then he had his gunfighter look with fancy clothes and a city slicker air about him. Now he had made clothing from hides of deer and elk—buckskin shirt, pants, jacket, and boots. He looked and acted like a fur trapper from high up in the mountains, and that was what he had turned into. Ron had long hair, a beard, and a coonskin hat. He also acted like an old mountain man who trapped animals for fur and lived like an Indian.

Life was good for him. He had learned how to survive in the forest, to hunt for food, and to find good water, and he also found a cave that he now called home. The cave had a perfect covered entrance and was high up on the mountainside, giving Ron a great view of the surrounding valley and mountainsides. Behind the cave was a nice meadow that was surrounded by very dense bushes, which concealed it perfectly. His horse could graze, and only God knew they were there. Plus, the thick bushes acted like a fence so the horse couldn't escape. *Perfect,* he thought when he started to eat the breast of the bird he had just roasted. It was very good too.

Ron sat there a long time after eating, thinking about the Crow he had seen a couple of weeks ago when they were going to bury Slippery Fish. He figured the dead Indian must have been native to this area for them to go this far for the burial. Slippery Fish must have been important to this area and held the high rank of chief or second brave. Ron wondered if they would be coming back to visit him in the future.

Tomorrow Ron would go scouting around the mountainside, looking down into the valley below. He thought it was time to check on the wagon train and maybe go and introduce himself. Should he or would that be stupid? He rolled out his bedroll, lay down, and fell fast asleep.

It was a beautiful night with the stars out so bright that they seemed like they were dancing and singing that the Great Spirit of God was in them. The moon was also bright, shining its light all over the earth. A night owl was heard screeching far off in the valley below. Gods animals were everywhere, feeding on the new grass and enjoying this time of plenty. The wind was blowing gently across the Plains and over the mountains.

The stream that ran past the settlers' new town played its own music, with the water running over the rocks and falling down in between them. Fish were jumping in the stream, making sounds that made you wonder what it was. All was at peace. Deer were in the meadow lying in the tall grass, with only one or two of them standing guard, watching for their enemies. It was warm for a springtime night. Tomorrow would be a good day too. It should be warm, sunny, and peaceful.

Ron was up before dawn to start his fire and cook breakfast. He would go scouting today to see if the settlers had left yet for the West. He would take along a bunch of jerky, his bedroll, and his cooking pans on his packhorse. Ron planned on being gone for a few days and wanted to be prepared. He would check out the settlers and see if there was a sign of the Crow. That thought sent a shiver up his spine, for they could be ruthless in war. But he needed to know where and what they were up to also. Traveling high above the others was an advantage for him as he could look down on them without being spotted. And he would make that even harder.

Ron started out a couple of hours later on his big horse. He thought about the forest, the mountains, the valley, and all the life around him when he started to think about God and how great he must be because he had made all this in a week. Wow!

That night, Ron camped next to a mountain stream that was at full flow down the side of the mountain toward the valley below. He had been looking for the settlers' camp all day and hadn't found it. *Tomorrow will be better,* he thought as he fell asleep.

The settlers were up and moving about the next morning, and little did they know that they were being watched. Ron had spotted them early in the morning and was just sitting on the mountainside, watching them as they went about their jobs. He was impressed with their little city with its tall, two-story town hall in the center. He watched as a hunting party rode out to the north and others went to the wooded area to start cutting down large trees. He assumed they were going to be logs for the fortress. They were planning on staying long term by the looks of it. *Should I continue to scout around or go looking for the Crow?* thought Ron as he stepped down off his horse. The Crow were nowhere to be found, which was strange. Ron wondered if the burial had something to do with their disappearance.

The old eagle was out today hunting when he decided to check in on the settlers too. He was surprised as Ron was when he saw the large city that had been built since the last trip here. He circled several times before he realized Ron was watching too. Now he wondered why. He had also missed the sparkle from Anna's necklace. She had her winter coat on now, so it could not be seen, but he knew she had it on.

Anna was walking across the campsite when she noticed the old eagle up above. He made her feel good because she looked at him like he was God's eyes watching over her. She always felt safe when she knew God was there, even though she knew the old eagle was just merely a sign of God. She had been busy every day with the common chores around the camp. *It is beautiful everywhere in the spring,* she thought as she walked toward the building in the center of the camp. Anna kept looking up to see if the old eagle was still flying around, looking down on them. At first, she didn't see him; but after a moment, she spotted him heading west again. Anna wondered if the old eagle lived alone or if he had a family when she remembered seeing a female flying with him last fall. Where was she now? *Maybe they have small ones at home now.* Then back to work she went.

The flowers were all over the meadow, just blowing in the wind, when Ron rode his beautiful big horse through it. When he looked in the direction he had come from, it looked like the trail was water parting in the sea when a vessel passed by. Ron was thinking about the beauty of God's handiwork when a flock of pheasants flew up out of the grass and scared him and his horse half to death. The horse had jumped sideways about six feet before he regained his composure and settled down again.

They were riding at the edge of some tall cliffs along the tree line on the mountainside near the settlers' camp. They were two thousand feet above the valley floor. When they were straight across from the campsite, he dismounted and tied his horse to a thicket of bushes and low-crawled to the edge of the cliff to see what was happening down below. He watched for nearly two hours before he decided to continue on scouting for the Crow or at least signs of them. The settlers' camp looked just like other camps he had seen before with nothing special except the big building in the center of the town. This made him think they were going to settle down right here. He wondered all afternoon about this and still was thinking when he rolled out his bedroll for the night.

Pete and Anna were walking across the campsite, holding hands, and talking about all that had happened to them in the last four years—Pete Jr.'s passing, the gathering of friends to move West, the hardships along the way, and now the campsite, which was rapidly turning into a small town.

It was pleasant to talk about now while walking slowly along and holding hands. This continued for more than a half hour, which to Anna seemed like and minute or two, for she loved this time alone with Pete when no one else could interrupt them. Pete enjoyed having her next to him as well. They both went into their wagon and fell asleep too.

All through the valley and the surrounding mountainside, the night had fallen on everyone and everything. The stars of heaven were dancing around as though they were showing off. The smell of spring was still in the air, aroused by a light wind blowing from the south. All was good tonight on God's earth.

The old eagle was high up in the tall pine tree, watching over his female friend while she was sitting on their eggs while waiting for a family.

The Crow had all crawled into their buffalo robes inside their tepees and were also sound asleep. Awanatu was lying there thinking about everything and wondered when he would be able to walk and ride like before. He was gaining strength daily and now had started walking again. *It won't be long before I'm riding again,* he thought. *And then I will show the palefaces who is the ruler of this part of the world.*

The night went fast like an egg through a hen or like a gas through a funnel. Morning was arriving now with the sun coming up over the mountains in the east. Far off in the distance, Ron heard a large rifle blast that sounded different from most rifles. It sounded like it carried a big slug with power. Then he remembered where and when he had heard that before. Back in his hometown in Kentucky, there was an old man who had lived out West during the buffalo-killing days, and he had a big rifle called the 1861 Henry. It bellowed like a cannon and would drop anything that it hit. He was wondering who would have an 1861 Henry out here.

Pete rode up to the big elk that he had just dropped with the 1861 Henry at three hundred yards. It had been a perfect shot through the heart, the size of a silver dollar going in and five times that size coming out of the other side. He started to field-dress the elk when Ole and a few of the guys rode up to see what he had shot as well as help him dress it out. They shared stories while they worked, and time seemed to fly by. They loaded a little bit on each horse and headed for camp.

The spring of 1870 was very beautiful, with the perfect amount of rain, sunshine, and wind. It was never too dry or too wet but just perfect. The flowers, grass, and small plants all around the meadows and forests were the best in many years.

Summer came in like a roaring lion with heat and more heat. The rain dried up completely, and so did the grass and the berries on the bushes. It was as though all were going to burn itself up and be no more.

The old eagle was busy providing for his family now. His female friend had hatched three chicks, two males and a female. The old eagle was hunting constantly around the clock. Hunting was hard because every animal in the land was struggling to survive. But that didn't matter now; he had to find something for all of them to eat, and that was what he did.

The settlers continued to build their town and the fortress around it while they looked for the Crow. Every day that passed without conflict made them feel more secure, thinking that maybe the Crow had forgiven them. The outer wall of poles stuck into the ground and sharpened at the top was complete. Now Ole and his gang were working on the big gates at each end of the fortress while the rest of them were laying a foundation for their new church. Life was good, even though it was so hot and dry. Hie stream continued to supply them a lot of water, which was also very good. They were hoping that the stream was good for all types of weather, and now they found out that it was. Very good.

Anna was caught several times a day by Pete with a worried look on her face. He would try to comfort her as much as possible, but it seemed to him to be useless. He was always happy to see her holding on to her necklace while walking through the camp because then he knew she was asking the higher power to help out.

Ron found that it was harder to find fresh berries, fruits, and wild cabbage in this drought. He was still having good luck finding game and having fresh meat. He was growing tired of the heat.

Oh-y-Yee was enjoying her time off from the grueling punishment of Awanatu now when he was regaining his health. Last spring, she realized she was gaining weight, so she started running hard each day by herself, pushing the limits. Now she was in the best shape of her life without a doubt. She would run as long as she could while kicking her heels in the air, in and around all the trees and small bushes at the edge of the meadows. Oh-y-Yee looked like a bodybuilder now with defined muscles on every part of her body. She was stunning to say the least.

Awanatu and the Crow were really healing fast now and were starting to practice war games again. They had not started on horseback yet, but it wouldn't be long before that would happen. The braves were practicing hand-to-hand combat along with different methods of killing and scalping their enemies. Next spring, they would avenge the people of the burial grounds by killing the palefaces who had wandered into their holy place of rest.

As summer turned to fall, the heat was lowered to a bearable level. The fall was very nice, just like the early spring had been. The only problem now was a shortage of wild berries and fruits for the settlers and the Crow. But the settlers had an advantage because of the big potato crop that they had because Ole had insisted that they plant them. Luck was with them this year.

In October, Old Man Winter came roaring in like a lion. On the fifteenth of the month came a very cold front down from Canada, pushing the temperature to a below twenty. High winds and blowing snow made it nearly impossible to withstand. This continued for almost a month before letting up for a couple of weeks. Then came the second blast from Old Man Winter, which was even colder and lasted longer. Spring would be beautiful when it came.

All across the High Desert country, winter was cold and wet with deep snowfall. The wildlife was having a hard time staying healthy, let alone alive. Everything and everybody was looking forward to next spring.

Oh-y-Yee and the Crow's herd of horses were spreading out farther and farther from the main camp, searching for grass. It was not good, nor was it plentiful, but it was all that there was to eat. Oh-y-Yee was working hard to keep in shape, but she knew she was losing some much needed weight because of lack of protein. Pine cones and pine needles helped out some along with tree bark, but they were the last resort for eating. This winter could be very long, and that could lead to some tough times before long. The winter of 1870 and 1871 was very cold, with high winds and more than normal amounts of snow. It was a good winter to have a lot of wood available, and that they did.

Anna had a surprise waiting for her early one morning in December when she went out of the wagon and heard little screams that sounded like newborn pups. Looking around, she found her German shepherd, Lady, with seven pups in a hollowed-out log next to their wagon. They were big pups that looked to be half wolf- gray, brown, and white mixed into one color called sable. They had dark masks on their noses and between the eyes.

Anna was so surprised and excited that she ran screaming toward the big building in the center of town while looking for Pete. Everyone was running from their wagons, thinking that the Indians were attacking, only to find Anna screaming about the new pups. Everyone had to come and look at them, and all of them thought they were cute and loving. Big Al warned everyone that they were wolf pups and that they could be the best protection they had, including their rifles. He went on to say that a wolf-cross pup would give them an early warning system because of their keen sense of smell and intelligence.

A couple of weeks went by, and Anna had selected the pup she wanted. He was the biggest pup with the darkest pigmentation around his eyes, making him look intimidating to say the least. She would name him Thunder. And he would grow up to be more than that name implied. He would grow to be thirty inches at the shoulder and weigh one hundred twenty pounds when lean. At three weeks of age, he was becoming tough as nails without any fear at all. She was sure that she had better teach him discipline early or not at all. Again, she was right.

In January, the winter settled down to normal amounts of snow and wind. All things were good again. By March, the Crow were starting to play their war games again. Awanatu had healed nicely, was trying to get back in shape, was riding Oh-y-Yee harder each day, and had now started training sessions twice a day. Both of them were getting stronger and better at what they had to do to be successful. It was hard work, but it had to be done.

The other braves were also working very hard to perfect their abilities of war. They were riding long distances at a fast pace to get the horses in shape, stopping quickly and reversing the direction to improve balance and quickness. It was a part of the big plan to have everyone and every horse in top shape for the long ride to the camp of the palefaces who had violated the burial grounds.

Oh-y-Yee and her herd mates were working harder than ever while preparing for war—running up hills at full speed, jumping over fallen logs, running through thick thickets of berry bushes while unsure of what was on the other side. All this was part of the plan. It was a grueling workout each day. The only good news was the fact that they all slept well at night.

Oh-y-Yee was thinking, while she was working so hard preparing for war, about the revenge she would soon have with Awanatu. She had a long list of things that could disable him or at least get him off of her back. Oh-y-Yee was planning on being free from his iron grip sooner than later, and she had to just figure out how to do that. Time would give her the advantage because the longer she was good to him, the more relaxed he would be, and that was when she would be free of his grip for good. She would need help because he was an excellent rider, and he seemed to know just when to lean one way or the other. Oh-y-Yee had also felt a slight pain in her ankle from the injury a year ago when she went over the cliff. It slowed her down on certain turns, so she was secretly trying to strengthen it.

Spring was rolling around again now, and the air was starting to smell like it. It was warmer now, and the grass was starting to poke its way up through the earth. Flowers, weeds, and trees were all starting to light up with new growth.

The old eagle was out flying around today, checking out the friends he had below. An hour ago, he had spotted Ron in a big meadow hunting deer that were constantly moving away from him. He was not happy.

Now the old eagle was flying over the settlers' new city, and he was impressed with all the building they had done. He saw Pete and Big Al walking across the compound and Ole and a group of men fixing a section of the wall that surrounded their city. Anna was also spotted along with her new pup, Thunder. The old eagle could see that the pup's father was a wolf. That could not be unnoticed. The pup had a wide, blocky head, which was a trait of the wolf. He thought that Anna had better know what she was getting into with him because, if she was not careful, the pup would become her worst nightmare soon.

He started flying back toward his nest now to see his young friend and sit on their eggs while she went hunting for their food. Their two chicks survived last year, and they were close by, so he could see them quite a bit, which made him happy. *Life is good,* he thought as he was flying along. Everyone and everything was at peace.

The next morning, he started flying early to the west to check on the Crow because it was around five hundred miles by air. The old eagle would take his time as he flew and therefore make it a two- or three-day trip.

As he flew along, he could see the new grass, bushes, and trees spouting their buds for the new year. The air was fresh and had a distinct smell to it. *God had done a great job when he made the world,* thought the old eagle.

While the old eagle was flying west, the Crow tribe was preparing for the spring hunt. When the moon came up at night with a full face, they knew it was time to hunt buffalo. They would be calving, and the new babies would slow the herd down, thus making the hunt easier. The Crow would only kill what they needed, and they would also use all of it without wasting anything. The meat would make jerky; the bones would be made into needles, knife handles, and so forth.

The night after the first hunt, the Crow would always have the feast of plenty. There would be dancing, music, and storytelling about the brave things that had been done during this hunt. Laughter and joy was plentiful as they thanked the Great Spirit of God. The Crow could see God all around themselves—in the mountains, streams, rocks, and water running downhill over and around the rocks. The Crow called it God's handiwork.

Nightfall came, and the Crow rested, and so did the old eagle. He found a large old pine tree that had a large branch sticking out. He landed on it because it would allow him to see all around without being seen himself. It was perfect. He too could sense God all around him. He felt safe knowing that God was watching out for him. He fell sound asleep almost immediately.

Early the next morning, he was flying west again with brisk flaps of his wings. He had rested well. As he approached the Crow nation, he noticed a large herd of buffalo grazing in a big green meadow just before entering Montana. There must have been thirty-five thousand of them. They were moving along at a fast pace, with many little calves running around while playing with one another. They were kicking up their heels and doing some head butting. Their mothers would look around for them every ten seconds or so, making sure they were okay.

Later that morning, the old eagle saw some mountain goats playing high up in the Rockies. They ran across the rocks off the valley floor like they had glue on their hooves, jumping and playing hide-and-seek while they kept one eye on their mother. *God has put common sense into their heads too,* thought the old eagle.

Soon the old eagle could see a column of smoke rising out of the forest about ten miles ahead of his location. This had him wondering who or what was causing the pillar of dust. It had to be someone or something running in a large group or herd to make a column this thick and tall. He would soon find out.

Chapter 16

The Crow had their horses on a full gallop through the forest like they were in a big hurry to get somewhere fast. It was a practice war with pretend white eyes who had very fast pretend horses. The Crow were so busy with the war games that they did not notice the slow-rising cloud of dust above the forest floor. Hiat cloud was rising higher and higher and was now becoming a sign for everyone to see, and it told a story.

Several miles away, a U.S. cavalry unit was working its way through the forest when they spotted the dust cloud high above the forest floor. They stopped, dismounted, and put their ear to the ground to listen for hoofbeats. And hoofbeats they heard, like many horses running very fast through the forest. Listening to the ground acted like a phone line by transmitting the sound clearer and faster than the air. Hie soldiers changed directions and started to approach the cloud of dust. They would need to find out what was going on over there.

Hie old eagle was flying high above, unnoticed as before. He could see the Crow and, to their left, the soldiers. He was old enough to understand the importance of the movements. Hie Crow were unaware, and the soldiers were aware but did not know who. This could spell disaster for one side or the other unless something changed and did it fast. The soldiers had increased their speed toward the dust cloud, causing another dust cloud to appear; and they, like the Crow, were unaware of it.

The old eagle looked back to the Crow when he realized their horses were painted for war with the dreaded hand inside the white circle and the feathers tied in the mane and tail of the horses. The braves also wore the dreaded hand painted on their cheekbones and on their quivers and shields. War was on the horizon for sure. Suddenly, the Crow stopped at a stream, suddenly cut to the right, and rode upstream against the current. This continued for several miles, which made the funnel cloud of dust disappear. They did not even notice, but the soldiers did, thinking the Crow had seen them and were planning an attack. Thus, the soldiers called off the pursuit.

The old eagle was confused as he flew, thinking about the events of the day. Where were the Crow going so fast, and why did they suddenly call it off? Soon he was flying directly overhead without being noticed. The Crow were heading toward home now; the old eagle watched them as they were walking slower up the stream. Soon they left the stream and headed into a meadow full of wild oats and rye. It had some beautiful flowers just swaying in the wind, with many colors present. *It is beautiful,* thought the old eagle as he noticed the soldiers turning back toward the direction they had come. Life was good.

They were at about six thousand feet of elevation where the wind was strong and the temperature nearly eighty degrees. All the braves dismounted after watering their horses, and now they were resting while the horses were grazing in the meadow. The braves were laughing and talking about who beat who during the war games. They were poking fun at a couple of braves who had made a sharp left turn when they should have turned right. Excited to tell their story, most of them tried to outtalk the others, while others just sat there listening and trying to divide the stories into truth and lies.

In the meadow, Oh-y-Yee was grazing alongside several other females while she was thinking about the events of the day. She had noticed that Awanatu had lost some of his power to hold on to her mane when making sharp turns to the right. She also noticed that his legs were not as tight and strong as they used to be. Maybe she could think about this and develop a plan to rid him from her back. Oh-y-Yee lay down now and fell into deep thoughts about her future. Hie other horses continued to graze all around the meadow. They had been worked very hard today, and they would sleep well tonight.

Awanatu was thinking about the day's events and wondering how he lost the strength in his arm and shoulder. His legs were also weaker than they had been, and now he had a worried look on his face. Deep thoughts were in his head about the future, which had been very bright but may be changing to a bleaker one. This worried him deeply.

Deer were grazing nearby, as well as elk and buffalo. Wolves were walking through the forest, looking for an animal in distress for their next meal. The birds were singing as they sat high up in the trees, away from danger. They would become very quiet when another animal entered the surrounding countryside. If that predator continued into the area, the birds would all together sound the alarm. Then the forest would go deathly silent. All the animals would freeze in their tracks while looking and listening for a predator in the area. When they were sure the threat was gone, they would sing loudly again.

The sound heard now was of water rushing downstream while hitting and sliding around rocks that made temporary blockages in the stream. It was a peaceful sound that brought ones mind to a neutral feeling concerning all things. A tune was played by the assorted sizes of rocks and how close they were to one another.

The wind was blowing slightly, but it whistled when the air went through the leaves on the trees. It continued at one pace for a few minutes, and then it would change to a higher speed for a while and then slow down or stop completely. Sometimes it would change directions for a moment or two and then continue from the same direction as before without any effort at all. Somewhere off in the distance, a wolf was howling; and many miles away, another answered. Life was good, and God was making music out here in the forest.

The old eagle was perched on a big branch high up in the tree he had chosen for the evening. It was swaying in the wind as well as rising and falling with the different gusts, making it a fun ride. He had this experience many times in his life, and he always thought it was fun. He was looking forward to tomorrow to see how all the people below would handle the stresses of the day. So now he was fast asleep, with his body moving with the rise and fall of the branch below him.

The sun was coming up over the mountains to the east with a bright smiley face and no wind anywhere. The day was going to be beautiful and slightly warmer than days before. Back at the wagon train, everyone was rising on this wonderful morning and starting the day's work. Hie women were preparing breakfast; the men were gathering wood or feeding the animals. Some of the men were harnessing the horses, getting them ready for another day's work of pulling logs around the outside of the camp or pulling wagons loaded with firewood into the camp for next winter. The children were helping wherever they could. Everyone was at peace and did not have a worry in the world. Or so they thought.

Ron was high up in the mountains hunting for deer when he heard hoofbeats coming down the trail toward him. He was scared for a moment, and then he left the trail and went into a thicket of gooseberry bushes and stood perfectly still for what seemed like forever. He was well hidden by all the stickily branches. He waited, and soon a group of settlers from the camp below went by his location in what seemed like a hurried pace. Ron was wondering, *Why the hurry? It is early in the day.* Ron waited an hour before he pulled out of the thicket and headed toward where the settlers had come. About an hour later, he found the reason the settlers had been in a big hurry to leave.

The grass was all mashed down in the meadow with blood and guts all over the matted grass. It looked as though a huge grizzly bear had been fighting over food when another bear had invaded his space, which led to a turf battle. Nothing is as dangerous as two giant male grizzlies fighting in a turf war. Smart people get out of the way. Ron thought that both bears must have had major injuries, so he would need to be on high alert for the rest of the day. A mad grizzly was very dangerous and would not stop until he was dead, and killing him would be very hard.

Anna was washing clothes down in the stream by rubbing them together while bringing them up from the stream and then back down into the water. It was a long and tedious job, but it had to be done. Her thoughts were wondering from Iowa to the West Coast and back. She was thinking about Pete Jr. and wondered how big he would be or what he would look like if he was still alive. Anna sure missed him every day and thought about him constantly. The clothes were almost clean now, and she was dreaming of their life in Iowa with little Pete while listening to the music being played by the water running over, under, and around the rocks in the stream. It was beautiful to hear.

Suddenly, there was a shout from behind her that scared her half to death. When she turned to see what or who it was, she saw Pete standing there laughing so hard that he could hardly stand. When he composed himself, he told her that it was nice to see her so content while washing his dirty old jeans and shirts. He asked her what she was thinking about for so long, and she responded by saying that it was little Pete, which brought a sullen and serious look from Pete. He thought for a moment, and then he said that he too had been thinking about little Pete, wondering what he would look like now and if he would be tall, strong, and handsome. They embraced and said they loved each other more now than ever. Pete picked up her basket of clothes, and they headed back toward the camp.

When they arrived at the camp, the members of the wagon train were all gathered around a fire while laughing, talking, and at the same time eating a piece of freshly killed buffalo meat. Some of the men were drinking homemade beer, and others were enjoying good old spring water. Everyone was having an enjoyable time, including the children, who were running, playing, and pretending to be a bad guy or an Indian. Tilings were good in the camp with plenty of food, water, and people to visit with. The place now looked more like a city than a camp along a stream. They had done well.

The old eagle was out today, enjoying the wind currents again. When the warm air from the ground started to rise, the old eagle would just float higher and higher with each minute, and soon the cool air would take him down to where he had started. It was soothing to the old boy, and it was effortless too.

He was looking down when he flew over the campsite, and he could hardly believe his eyes. The camp looked twice as big as before with many new buildings. The settlers were working down below, with many of them around the big campfire in the center of the town. It looked like all was going well for them. He wondered if the Crow were still planning for revenge or if time had softened their hostile attitudes. *I would have to check on them soon,* he thought.

Seven hundred miles away, the Crow were back to practicing war again. Riding hard for extended periods, shooting arrows from horseback, throwing spears and javelins, and jumping off a running horse and swinging back on them were also being done. The braves were getting into great shape, and their horses were even better.

Oh-y-Yee was in the best shape of her life. She could run all morning long with ease while thinking of how she would rid herself of Awanatu. He was not as strong as he used to be, and she knew it. So did he.

Her plans were becoming clearer and clearer each day now. Oh-y-Yee would wait until they were in the heat of battle before she would act. Then it would be sudden and swift. She was sure she would be able to sense the time or object that would help her decide how to rid her of him, and she would be ready. In the meantime, she was working very hard to become stronger and faster than ever before.

The wind had picked up now, and it was blowing her mane and tail in swirling circles, making it look braided. It felt good to have that wind blowing but not now when it was picking up dust and throwing it in her eyes, making them burn and start tearing them up. There wasn't anything you could do about it except tear up until the water running down your face would wash the eyes out completely. By then, there were more dust, grass, and debris blowing into them. Oh-y-Yee decided that the only thing to do was to seek a ravine to hide in until the wind stopped, so that was what she did.

To her surprise, the ravine was full of Crow ponies hiding from the wind with their heads down toward their feet. This protected their eyes from flying dust and debris that could blind a horse and that would spell the end for them, and the Great Spirit had given them this instinct. They would stay here until the wind died down or stopped.

Many of the Crow ponies thought Oh-y-Yee was the greatest horse of all time. They moved out of her way when she walked by them, showing her the most respect a horse could show for another horse. They could see how big and strong she was and therefore didn't even try to challenge her in any way. Most of the stallions were afraid of her strength and power too. She was the queen, and she knew it.

Oh-y-Yee had decided, a few weeks ago, that she would work harder than ever to be in the best shape of her life because she was sure the Crow would soon attack the settlers and to rid herself of Awanatu. And that couldn't happen fast enough for her. Since his accident, he had held the complete blame on Oh-y-Yee for going over the cliff and landing on him. He had become harsh and blunt in his corrections and would ride her harder than ever before. She did not like that treatment at all. *Vengeance will he mine sooner or later,* she thought.

The old eagle had headed west to the Crow nation when the wind picked up, and he had thus found a big old jasper pine tree with an exposed branch about forty feet from the ground to roost on for the night. As he sat there, he fell into a deep sleep with wild dreams of the Crow riding hard toward the settlers with the dreaded hand painted on their horses and the left side of their faces. The old eagle could see they were carrying many arrows, knives, and spears. They were out to bring revenge to the settlers for the dead from the burial grounds. The settlers would pay for their sins against the dead. Just then, a strong wind current came from below and up through the branches and almost blew him out of the tree. He was instantly awake. Then he realized that he had been dreaming and went back to sleep.

Around midnight, the wind died down, the clouds were gone, and a bitter cold front set in from the north. The temperature dropped twenty-five degrees in two hours, making it a very chilly night for this time of the year. The old eagle couldn't wait until morning to get rid of the bitter chill running through his bones. *Sooner or later, it will come,* he thought as he drifted off to sleep again.

Oh-y-Yee and the other Crow ponies were down in the ravine waiting until morning, even though the wind had died. They knew all too well that the ravine would also be warmer than the open meadows for the night. So they just stayed put. The Crow were all in their tepees with a roaring fire going, which made them very comfortable and almost hot. They could hear the wind blowing earlier, and they were also thinking they were lucky to be in camp inside the tepees tonight.

Seven hundred miles east of the Crow camp were the settlers in their village. They had really built a nice city with great walls, buildings, and a protection plan in case of an Indian attack. Most people wouldn't even know it was the same place they were at a year ago. It was impressive to see.

Pete, Anna, and Big Al were all sound asleep in their buffalo robes, lying around their campfire, soaking in the warm air. They had been chilled to the bone earlier in the evening when the wind was howling through the campsite at forty miles per hour. It had made the dust fly in their eyes and dirt in their hair and the wood in the campfire burn twice as fast without any extra heat.

Anna was now lying there awake, thinking about their past in Iowa and then Pete Jr. She wondered how he would look now, if he would be tall and lean or stocky and strong. She would never know, but that didn't stop her from wondering. Anna kept thinking about him until she fell asleep. Tomorrow would be another day, and then they would see what the weather was like to plan their day.

The next morning, as the sun was rising over the mountains to the east, it cast long shadows of trees and sharp, jagged peaks against the ground. It was almost scary to look at because it made shapes that moved when the wind blew. It was going to be hot today, but if the wind kept blowing, it wouldn't seem so bad.

Chapter 17

Ron was awake and out in front of his cave building a fire with some dried cedar branches that had fallen off the trees last fall and were very dry. The cave had become his home, and he loved it. If it was raining, he would build his fire just inside the cave, and then the smoke would leave the cave, swirl up along the wall of stone, and spread so that it couldn't be seen from the outside. He had found a little spring of water around the corner from the entrance, and he had dug a trench to the edge of the cave. There, he had dug a little lake for the water to stay in before it ran out to the other side and down the hill. He had fresh running water all year round. It was great.

Inside the cave, he had divided it into several rooms. It branched out in three directions twenty feet inside the cave's entrance. The tunnel to the left was his bedroom, where he had fixed a nice bed made from pine limbs and branches. He had fastened a small limb on the cave wall and then carved a spot on the limb that held a nice big candle. He had light at night; plus, it was cozy. Hie homemade gun rack hung up on the wall by his bed, and it had room for three big rifles and a peg to hang his holsters. It looked good to him, and it was warm at night as well as cozy.

Hie middle room was where he stored his meat. He had elk, moose, and deer shanks, ribs, and hindquarters hanging from the ceiling in this part of the cavern. He also stored firewood for the winter and some carrots, potatoes, and other root plants that needed a cool, dry place for storage. It was dry and remained a constant fifty-six degrees year round. Hie meat would age as it dried, and sooner or later, it would become jerky if he hadn't eaten it fast enough. Most of it had a generous amount of salt spread on it to prevent it from becoming green with mold.

Hie last section was where he stored hay for his horses, saddles, and pack gear. He also had made a couple of stalls for his horses to keep them inside during the terrible storms that could come through the mountains at any time. He liked his cave, and it was very homey.

Hie cave was very protected from the outside as well. It was very hard to find, with the big cedar trees all around the front of it forming a natural barrier and looking like no one could find access to anything but a large wall of stone. It was hidden from all viewpoints. Hie only entrance was from the rear of the cedars on the right-hand side of the cave. There was not even the sign of a path leading to the entrance because the ground was solid rock for five hundred feet in all directions, impossible to find unless you accidently stumbled onto it.

Ron had cut a piece of meat off the hanging elk and was now roasting it slowly over the fire. He was letting his thoughts go wherever they wanted to go, and that they did. He had been here a couple of years now, but it seemed longer than that to him. Ron totally enjoyed his home and surroundings. He looked upward and saw the smoke from the campfire rising slowly along the rock wall above the entrance to the cave, spreading itself out as it rose high on the cliff. By the time it reached the top, it had spread so wide that no one could even see it.

He was now eating some of the elk meat and sitting at the edge of the cedar trees in front of the cave while watching the sun slowly settle in the west. *It is great to be alive,* he thought as the sun settled below the horizon in the west. Soon another day would be over, and tomorrow he would start all over again. Each day was a battle just to survive out here in the wild.

Then he started thinking about his past and wondered if he would be in Boot Hill now had he not traveled out West. Ron was just sure that someone would have killed him, or he would be in prison now. Hiat set of thoughts scared him, and he abruptly dismissed all of them quickly. Ron wanted to dismiss his past and had asked the great God above to forgive him of all the evil he had committed before this day. He felt forgiven and was forgiven, for the Bible told him so. Ron carried a little Bible everywhere he traveled, and he read it daily.

Ron had learned how to tan hides and sew the pieces together to make shirts, pants, boots, and all other types of leather items like a knife sheath and saddlebags. He was proud of his work and latest look, which was like a mountain man and trapper. Not only did he look like it but he also had changed into just that, a mountain man and trapper.

His horse was in the small meadow behind the cave, which was completely shut in by big groups of gooseberry bushes so thick that a man could not see through them, nor could anyone ride or walk through them. It was a perfect spot for concealing the horse while it grazed. He did not have to hobble the horse when it grazed either because of the thickets. Along with the hidden front view of the cave, this could not have been planned better than it was already. This place was perfect.

All through the land, everyone and everything was now lying down to sleep for the night except the predators. Hieir day was just starting, and they had a big advantage with their night vision. Hieir sense of smell, night vision, and big sharp teeth gave them a huge advantage. Off in the distance, a wolf was howling; and farther off, he was answered by another. Coyotes could also be heard but in submission to the wolf.

The stars were out bright with a full moon overhead like it was looking down to see what was going on in the world. The wind was blowing from the northwest, and it would get colder tonight than previously. It was a good night to have a buffalo robe and a good fire roaring well into the night.

The smell in the air this morning was of fall. One could smell the difference in the smell of the cedars, pines, and the grass. It was hard to explain, but if you had lived in the wilderness, you would know the difference. It was ten degrees colder than yesterday, but it was sunny without a cloud in the sky. The leaves on the trees seemed to be changing their colors just slightly, but soon they would be dressed in fancy red, yellow, and purple colors. Old Man Winter was coming again soon.

The tall old pine tree far up on the mountainside had been the home of the old eagle for nearly twenty years now. He had raised many offspring in this old tree. He was getting older and slower, but he still enjoyed checking in on his humans in the world below him. This morning, he was just going to fly toward the settlers to see what was new or changed in their lives. That would be interesting to him. He thought he would just fly down there and snoop around for a while, find a nice tall tree and rest for the night, and then find his way home tomorrow.

Off in the distance, he could see the campsite, and it looked bigger and better than ever before. New buildings were scattered around it, and in the center of the camp was a tall windmill. It was pumping water into a large water trough beneath its tall frame. It looked like a blacksmith shop was built in the southwest corner of the camp, and it had a large stable attached that looked like it held thirty horses.

The old eagle was impressed with what he had just seen down below. Wow, *they have been working hard around here,* he thought as he flew in a large circle, allowing the wind currents to lift him and then drop him suddenly as if he would continue until he hit the ground. *The air currents are always fun.*

His mind went off into another direction, thinking of the power that the Great Spirit must have. *Where did the wind come from, and where did it go?* he wondered as he floated along, looking at the ground.

Now the old eagle decided to head for home, and as he was flying to the southwest along the foothills, he caught a glimpse of a sparkle. He looked off to the north, and he recognized the sparkle; it was the necklace of Anna with the picture of little Pete in the heart-shaped locket. The old eagle was sure Anna would be holding it and rubbing it as though little Pete would feel better when she did that.

He turned his head to the south and remembered Ron, the mountain man who lived over the steep cliff on this side of Mount Killdeer. Ron had showed up out of nowhere dressed like a gunfighter but soon changed to a full-blown mountain man. He would fly over the area where he had seen Ron before to see if he could spot him again.

Soon the old eagle was flying over the treetops near where he had seen Ron before and started wondering where Ron lived. He had not seen a tepee, a cabin, or a tent ever now that he thought about it a bit. It made him more curious than ever. The old eagle searched for over an hour and found no sign of Ron, his horse, or anything that was his. Then he looked for trails to and from the streams and pastures with signs of horses in them or trails, but there was none. *How could a man live here and not show a sign of himself or his horse anywhere?* wondered the old eagle. *Ron is a mystery.* And he flew toward home.

Ron had mastered the art of living in one area for a long time without being noticed. His hidden cave, the solid rock floor all around it, the bushes in front that concealed it, the thicket-fenced pasture out back, and the spring-fed pond just inside the entrance to the cave were instrumental in his being unnoticed in the mountains near the settlers below the mountain. He was planning on keeping it this way for a long time too. He was careful to choose a different path every time he left the cave to go somewhere else on the mountain. He came back to the cave by another route each time as well. Caution would protect him.

That night as Ron lay on his homemade bed with a buffalo robe as a mattress, he started thinking about his survival. He had gone unnoticed for several years now, and he wondered how long it would stay that way. In his mind, he was double-checking everything he had been doing while wondering if he could improve it. Yesterday he had spotted an eagle soaring overhead for a long time, and Ron thought he could feel some eerie presence about that eagle. It was almost like the eagle was trying to figure out where and how Ron went unnoticed for so long. He was thinking about this an hour later as he fell asleep. Later that night, he was dreaming about covering his tracks every time he left the cave or came back to it. Many thoughts came and went during his dream.

The Crow had a busy, long, and hard summer. They had prepared for war and revenge against the settlers, winter, and the normal things of the day. They were tired and would need the winter to rest and make new arrows, spears, and bows. They had gathered all the wild rose stems for making arrows and spears. Now they would have to trim and heat them, and then they could straighten every one of them. It was slow and slower.

The nights were getting colder and longer now, and the north wind blew stronger and was colder. The fires in the tepees were hot and never would grow cold until next spring. It was peaceful to say the least. The entire Crow nation had been busy all summer and fall preparing for a long winter, even though one may not be long and cold. It was better to be prepared than not to be because you would starve in a long winter. In the past, there had been close calls where food supply had run out before the winter ended, but they were lucky enough to catch fish, rabbits, and fowl to survive.

They had made a vast supply of bows, arrows, knives, and spears this past winter and spring in preparation of the upcoming war against the wagon train. The Crow had also practiced many hours on horseback, playing war games in which they conquered the settlers each time. The braves made many daring moves from horseback, on foot, and in hand-to-hand combat. They rehearsed the moves over and over until each brave knew it by heart and could not fail. The Crow and their horses were in the best shape of their lives and ready for war.

Oh-y-Yee was also in the best shape she had ever been in, with her body rippling with toned muscle. She was faster and quicker than ever before too. None of the other females were even close to her in body build and shape. They were smart enough to never challenge her in any way because they knew it would not be good for them in any way, shape, or form. Oh-y-Yee was the queen, and she knew it.

All spring and summer, she was thinking of a way to destroy Awanatu, and now she had a plan. Next spring, it would be put into effect. She couldn't wait until it happened. Awanatu was in for the surprise of his life.

Fall turned to winter one day early in November when the wind changed suddenly from an eastward direction to a wind coming straight down from Alaska in the north. The temperature dropped twenty-five degrees in less than twenty minutes, and it felt horribly cold compared with the day before. Before nightfall, it started to snow; and with the wind blowing this hard, there would be large drifts in the morning.

Fall and winter left as fast as they came. It was now March 23. The snow was melting, and the air around them was getting warmer and also smelled cleaner and fresh. Now the demanding work drills continued just as before winter. The braves were riding the horses harder, longer, and faster than ever before. Not only were the drills hard but they also were twice a day for at least four hours. In the evenings, both the Crow and their horses were extremely tired and dirty. War games were very hard to play in the spring when the dirt was soft or mud, but they did it the same way as before when it was too hot and dry.

Oh-y-Yee was working harder than ever to get into and stay in shape. She was planning what she thought was the end of her relationship with Awanatu. Daily she was possessed by the thoughts of accomplishing this feat. Time would tell about how it would happen.

She was big, strong, and amazing to look at with her beautiful dapple-gray color pattern. When looking at her, you could see immediately that she was special, not only in form and strength but also in intelligence. And intelligent she was. When running during the war games, Oh-y-Yee was also planning how she would, once and for all, get rid of Awanatu. Her power and solid frame was impressive when she was standing still but even more impressive when she was running while thinking of the plan that would free her forever.

Tonight after a grueling day of war games, she went to a place in the meadow where the grass was all gone, leaving only a dry area filled with dust. There, she went down on her front knees and lay down. Then she rolled over onto her back and wiggled back and forth until she was completely covered in mud and dust and had lost all her beautiful dapple-gray color. Now she had turned into an ugly blond-gray/brown color that had spots that were still wet and dark. Hiis was how horses dry off after a rough day of challenging work. After this ritual, she joined the rest of the horses in the meadow, grazing.

The Crow were all gathered around the campfire, roasting fresh deer meat while talking in excited voices of the days work and what was impressive during the day. Awanatu and Oh-y-Yee were the highlight of all discussions. Oh-y-Yee received more comments than he did, and that did not set well with him. As a matter of fact, that made him furious with her, and tomorrow he would ride her harder than ever before and make her look bad. His number one downfall would be his eagerness to get revenge. No one gains anything by seeking evil on another being, for that right belongs only to God himself.

He was thinking she needed to know he was the boss, and tomorrow he would show her. The next morning, Awanatu was up before sunrise, getting everything ready for a grueling day of training with Oh-y-Yee. He was determined to show her who the boss was, and this he would do by riding her hard and fast with many turns, stops, and starts until she could hardly walk without trembling.

Oh-y-Yee could see Awanatu walking briskly across the meadow toward her with a grim look on his face. She had seen that look before, and it meant it would be an exhausting long day. Nothing would be overlooked and everything evaluated in a negative manner. For a moment, she thought about running from him as he approached, but she knew that would only lead to more nastiness from Awanatu. Instead, she submitted, and he led her toward the camp.

Campfires were going strong now, the wood was crackling and spitting coals out of the fire circle, and the air had the smell of freshly roasted meat in it. The aroma was very good. It had the same smell seven hundred miles to the east by the campfires of the settlers. Coffee had a very strong smell there while the meat was second, with a wonderful seasoned aroma from the old hickory wood used to roast it. Hie fires were just blazing all around the campsite, and the settlers' families were starting to come outside toward the fires to be with their loved ones. The sun was coming over the mountains in the east, and it was stunning just to look at for a while.

Anna was standing in the court square looking at the sunrise, with her thoughts ruling her body completely. She was motionless. Her thoughts were of her son, Pete Jr., wondering how he liked heaven, if he missed her, and if they could have done anything different to change the outcome of what had happened. After several minutes there alone with her thoughts, the silence was broken by Big Al's voice when he asked, "A penny for your thoughts?" She did not answer him as she hurried toward the big fire in the center of the courtyard, so he did not see the tears running down her face.

Soon Pete came around the corner, stopped to talk to Big Al, and spotted Anna near the main campfire. He turned and was heading straight toward her when Al grabbed his arm and said, "Careful. Anna was here crying before I came out. When I asked her about her thoughts, she left crying and trying not to be noticed. I don't know what that was about, but I would guess it was about little Pete again." Pete was wondering when she would be able to let it go as he walked toward her.

Anna looked toward Pete with swollen eyes, and then the tears started flowing again. She leaned on Pete's shoulder and cried until she couldn't anymore. Then Anna felt better, and Pete was relieved and confused.

Pete joined a group of men around the main town hall who were talking about the fortification of the campsite. He heard Ole say that they had spotted several Crow pony hoofprints on the trail just north of the stream by the camp. He was sure they had better fortify the camp and do it quickly. All the men thought they needed a meeting as soon as possible to discuss the fortification. They all agreed to meet tomorrow evening.

This spotting of Indian pony hoofprints in the ground on the other side of the stream will definitely bring some discomfort and fear, thought Pete as he walked through the little city. What could they do about it? It was exactly what Ole had said—fortifications.

Pete's thoughts were wandering all day long as he worked. He was thinking about the hoofprints and wondered which Crow Indian they belonged to and how many different ponies had been there in the last month or two. It was important to know who, how many, and when. *Time will tell,* he thought, but in the meantime, they had better start the fortifications.

Chapter 18

High up on the side of the mountain above the settlers' camp stood a big, strong, dapple-gray mare. She had been ridden hard for a long time because she was covered in dust on her sweaty hair and hide. She looked tired and was gaunt from not being able to eat enough grass lately. Even though she had been ridden hard and long, her strength was evident, and her shape was outstanding. One could see she was a one-of-a-kind mare—the best of the best. Seventy-five yards to her left, fifteen Crow ponies were tied in a thicket of wild cedar trees while resting from the hard long ride. They were of good quality but not the same as the dapple- gray mare named Oh-y-Yee.

Back on the bluff overlooking the settlers' camp below stood Oh-y-Yee, who was standing perfectly still, while her rider was looking back and forth, up and down, and all around the campsite below, looking for a weakness in their fortification. He was very strong and young with good looks and had a distinct air about him. Awanatu was frustrated because he could not find an obvious weakness, and that made him more persistent in his search. Finally, he sent six braves down the mountainside to scout the campsite up close to see if they could find any. He turned Oh-y-Yee away from the bluff toward the Crow ponies tied in the thicket. There, they would wait for the braves to come back and report on what they had discovered down below.

In the campsite, Anna had this uneasy feeling of being watched all day long. It seemed as though someone was standing behind her while looking over her shoulder. Many times, she had turned around to find nothing different from the last time she had looked. But she continued to check until she found Pete, and then she started to cry and cry as she did when her nerves were shot. When she settled down, she told Pete of her feelings, and he said he had felt the same. Pete told Anna he would send several men up onto the mountainside to check for anything that looked strange or different from before. Pete planned to do this first thing in the morning.

The Crow braves were now heading up the mountainside to report back to Awanatu. They had found no weakness in the encampment either. The settlers had everything built very strong with thick logs and timbers, and they were bolted together with big steel bolts and long steel spikes. It looked impossible to have an advantage over the settlers with this big strong fortification. The braves were sure that Awanatu would not be happy with their report. They were trying to figure out who would do the reporting as they rode up through the steepest part of the mountainside, which was covered with cedar trees and small thickets of gooseberry bushes. It was nearly impossible to get through, and if you did, you would have plenty of scratches and cuts, which they did.

Oh-y-Yee was tired of standing still for such a long time while waiting for the braves to return. She had evil thoughts about her rider while she stood motionless waiting. *Now is not the time,* she thought.

Suddenly, they appeared covered with cuts and scratches and looking very tired. Awanatu perked up and kicked Oh-y-Yee in the ribs, and she lunged forward so fast that he almost lost his balance and fell to the ground. But he recovered very quickly, and she was surprised again. They were talking very fast and in an excited tone. Awanatu was upset and started yelling at the braves, and she could see they were nervous about what they had said. Finally, Awanatu turned her head abruptly, kicked her in the sides, and headed to the encampment where the ponies had been tied by the long thicket of small trees and bushes.

The next morning, the settlers' scout party started tracking the Crow ponies as the trail led toward the mountainside and then started up it. Henry Stahl led the party, and after a while, he stopped, and they began to talk. Henry thought there were ten to twelve ponies that they were tracking; the group believed it was twelve of them. By midday, they were making slow progress and were only a third of the way up the steep slopes, arriving at the cedar trees and thickets. *It will get slower now,* thought Henry.

A Crow scout came into camp quickly and was excited. Soon after he finished talking, the group gathered all their belongings and headed west fast. Oh-y-Yee knew what had happened. The settlers had discovered the Indian pony hoofprints and were now tracking them. The Crow had to leave because they were not prepared for a battle. And leave they did as fast as their horses could carry them. It was fairly easy traveling at this altitude because of very few trees and bushes to slow one down. It also was hard to track them because of the partly frozen ground. After a few hours, the Crow had gained enough ground on Henry Stahl's group to slow down and take it easy on their horses. Oh-y-Yee and the other ponies were worn out and instantly slowed down to a nice walking pace.

Henry Stahl and his group had now reached the spot on the side of the mountain where the Crow had camped for a couple of days. They counted the hoofprints of the horses and came up with ten light pony hoofprints and a larger one that they were sure belonged to the horse of a chieftain or high-ranking brave. *It must have been from a very big strong horse,* they thought as they expressed their opinions about all that they had found. They could see imprints on the ground where the Crow had rested, and they counted eleven such spots in the soil. Now they knew they had the upper hand if it came to a battle. Henry knew the Crow wouldn't have any big buffalo guns that could fire rapidly and most likely only had arrows, spears, and knifes, so he decided to pursue the Crow for a couple of days just to scare them away for a while so the settlers could prepare the encampment to withstand an attack.

The Crow found one of their favorite hideouts that was located on a steep side of the mountain that, in turn, was covered with small bushes that had long and sharp thorns on the branches. Unless you knew where to enter, you could not find your way into the center of the brush, where there was a big open space to camp without anyone finding you.

Soon after they ate, they rolled out the buffalo hides, lay down, and went to sleep. Awanatu started to dream, but it felt lifelike to him. The great warrior Slippery Fish came to him in a dream to give advice about the pale-faced men and women of the wagon train. He started by saying that the Great Spirit had sent him to warn him of the dangers ahead if he chose to attack the settlers. Slippery Fish looked very impressive, almost perfect in form, muscle, and shape. He had all his war paint on when he began his speech. He said, "The Great Spirit sent me to tell you the dangers of going to war with the pale-faced people. They have many big guns, a strong fortress, and enough food and water to last many moons. The Great Spirit wishes you would forgive and make peace, and if you don't, bad medicine will fall upon you and the others. This was promised to me by him."

As he was talking, he began to start wiping the war paint off his face as a sign of the peace he felt in his heart. Then he said, "The Great Spirit said they didn't know that they were trespassing on the holy ground, and therefore, you should forget and forgive them."

Awanatu continued dreaming for over an hour and then woke up in a cold sweat. He was scared for the first time since childhood. He remembered everything that Slippery Fish said and how he said it. Awanatu felt very alone and small now after the lecture from Slippery Fish, who was a hero of the Crow because of his wisdom and kindness toward all others. Then he was wondering why the Great Spirit had sent Slippery Fish to warn him of the danger that lay ahead. Was it because he was heading in the wrong direction, or could there be another reason? He would think about this dream appearance for months to come, going over and over it, trying to figure it out completely.

Oh-y-Yee woke up during the night and thought she heard voices coming from the bedroll of Awanatu. It was like a spirit voice that was sweet and soothing. It continued for a long period, almost like a speech from a higher authority. Awanatu had spoken several times but was quickly stopped by the spirit person and told to listen, and that he did quickly. Then Oh-y-Yee thought she had seen a bright flash of light, and all of it was over instantly as the spirit person disappeared.

The next morning, Awanatu was visibly shaken by the appearance of Slippery Fish the night before. He didn't want to listen to the speech from the spirit world, but that was hard to do. It bothered him all morning, and he was glad they were riding all day, so he could think about what had been told to him. He was scared and shaken and felt hopeless to find the correct answer to the speech delivered by Slippery Fish. Awanatu also felt deep resentment from the speech and toward the settlers as he thought they should be punished for their sins against the Crow holy burial site. He wanted revenge badly.

Oh-y-Yee could see that he was bothered too. And she knew why. There had been a spirit-filled person with Awanatu the night before, and she wondered who appeared or what had been said that shook him so badly. She could see that his face was drawn tight, and worry lines were everywhere.

Meanwhile, Henry Stahl had stopped pursuing the Crow braves because they had outdistanced Henry and his men. There was no point in chasing them further, so they turned back toward the settlement. As they rode along, Henry started thinking about what had happened in the last three or four days. We *need to start having sentries a mile out from the settlement 24/7,* he thought. They would also need a way to warn the settlers if the Crow were approaching and from which direction they were coming. They needed a system quickly because now they had been warned by the appearance of the Crow scouting out the settlement. Fortifications also needed to be in top shape with plenty of food, water, and supplies available. They needed to call a meeting soon and make some plans, both short term and long term. Henry and his group were heading back to the settlement, and so did the Crow.

The old eagle was now out flying again, circling the Crow Indian camp, and he could see that the war party had arrived home. The old eagle wondered where they had been and why. This made his mind go faster and faster while wondering what was going on. He circled and found Oh-y-Yee in the meadow with the other ponies; they looked tired, and all of them were resting on the grass, with some of them flat out. They had been on a long journey, and he wondered if they had attacked the settlers. That was where he would be going next. So he headed east in a hurry to find out more news about what was happening.

That night, the old eagle was more than halfway to the settlers' campsite when he found a large tree to spend the night, roosting high up on a large branch that reminded him of home. He slept well and woke up to a bright, sunshiny day. It was beautiful as a fresh rain had arrived overnight, making everything smell wonderful. He thanked God and started eastward toward the settlers.

When the old eagle was ten miles from the settlers' camp, he looked down and saw Henry Stahl and his group riding toward camp at a higher rate of travel than what was normal. He sensed the excitement in their motions. The old eagle was wondering, *What has happened, and why are they out here riding back toward the settlement with such speed?* He continued to fly onward to the settlement, where everything looked normal as could be except there were less men in camp. *They are with Henry.*

Before long, Henry Stahl and the group of men riding with him entered the camp from the western end. The people were excited to see them and gathered around them, talking in loud voices. The old eagle could tell they were worried, excited, and anxious to hear what had happened west of the village. The settlers and the Crow Indians were all excited and, at the same time, worried about their future, even though they were separated by miles of prairie.

The old eagle decided to fly to the southern side of the valley on his way home to see what Ron was doing up high in the mountains near his cave. Once he was overhead, he spotted Ron out in front of his cave skinning a large elk. He looked happy and well fed. Now the old eagle continued toward the large jasper pine he had called home for over sixteen years. He was looking forward to seeing his young sweetheart and their young eagles, which were only two and a half months old. All the action in the valley below would have to wait until he had more time to spend looking around and observing.

The settlers had their meeting, and they implemented several changes in the security of the camp—more guards two miles out in all four directions with signals to alert the camp if the Crow were coming, with two men at each location. They started building stronger barriers around the compound, which included big, strong, and thick gates on three sides of the village. They also were constructing high towers at the end of each of the walls so they had a clear view of the walls and surrounding landscape. Hedgerows made of stone and concrete four feet high and angled in different directions were also planned so the Crow would not be able to get in close while on a full gallop. Many things were happening all at once because they understood the fact that their survival depended on it. They decided to work very hard to fortify their settlement and to do it fast.

Meanwhile, the Crow were practicing war games every day, working their horses and the braves very hard to develop stamina. The skills of the braves were improving daily and fast. Awanatu decided to ignore Slippery Fish's warning, thinking he was smarter, stronger, and better than any dead old Indian, even if he had been well respected while here on the earth.

The next four months passed quickly while both groups worked very hard with long hours to accomplish their pursuits. It was midsummer now, and the Crow were ready to head east to attack the settlers' village. Awanatu was now calloused to the point that he was sure they could take out the settlers and avenge the trespassing of the holy burial grounds. The mistake that had been made was Awanatu didn't know the settlers were also busy during the last four months. The camp had changed so much that you wouldn't know it was the same campsite as four months ago.

The Crow headed eastward toward the settlers' camp thinking, laughing, and telling tall tales of how they would kill and take many scalps. It almost held a party attitude. They had over two hundred warriors all with war paint on themselves and their horses. The quivers were full of arrows, the knives were sharpened, and so were their spears. The shields were hanging on the sides of their horses made from stretched buffalo hides that dried to a very hard surface; these could stop most small-caliber bullets. They and their horses were all painted with a circle around the eyes, the dreaded hand on their face or rump, and their weapon of choice on the other cheek. Feathers were also in their hair and in the mane and tails of the horses. They looked as ready as ever.

Oh-y-Yee's heart raced as she thought of the upcoming war with the settlers. This could be her chance to rid herself of Awanatu forever if she thought of a good way to do it long enough. She was in the best shape of her life, and she knew she had an advantage over him after the terrible accident where he had been hurt so bad that he almost died.

Two days later, as Ole Olson and Harold Hammerslund were on duty guarding the western side of the campsite, they heard horses coming, and it sounded like a lot of them. They were Indian ponies because they could not hear horseshoes clanking against rocks. They were hidden well and could not be detected easily. They watched through the thicket and saw the warriors going past their hiding place in single file. It was scary to say the least, with all the war paint covering them and their horses.

The lead horse was a big strong dapple-gray mare with outstanding form and muscles to no end. She was impressive as was her rider, a brave who held a high rank in the Crow nation, Ole and Harold were sure. They watched as the braves filed past, with Ole looking at their weapons and Harold counting the braves and their horses. The last few braves led some extra horses and a few carrying supplies but not much other than dried jerky and blankets. When the last of them had filed by, Harold said there were 216 braves, and Ole said they only had bows, arrows, knives, and spears for weapons, plus three old U.S. Army rifles that were known to jam when fired more than once a minute.

Now Ole and Harold had to warn the camp of the impending battle, so Ole went south for a couple of miles and then headed east as fast as his horses could go, while Harold went north a mile and then east fast. This way, if the Crow were to stop one of them, the other would make it safely to the camp. Ole and Harold were traveling as fast as they could, while the Crow were going slow so as not to disturb the wildlife that could alert the settlers of a stranger in the neighborhood.

When Ole and Harold were within eyesight of the camp, they fired two shots into the air as a warning to the villagers. It also alerted the other guards to come to the fortress quickly, and that they did. Once inside the walls, all the inhabitants took up their positions around the walls and towers. Some were to fire guns toward the invaders and others to reload or help the wounded. They were ready.

Then the Crow appeared; they were so impressive as were their ponies, all painted with the dreaded hand to match the braves' paint. They must have stopped and wiped the sweat from the horses before lining up to show their strong presence. They all lined up on the west and south sides of the camp just outside the range of the rifles except for the 1861 Henry buffalo gun.

Now is the chance of a lifetime, thought Big Al and Pete as they leaned their big 1861 Henrys on the top of the wall, took aim, and shot an Indian each toward the center of the group. Both Indians fell backward off their horses and hit the ground dead. The Crow were totally shocked that the gunfire could reach them and retreated immediately. Now all the settlers were ready for the attack, with all guns ready to fire when the Crow came; but before they gathered their guts to charge, another surprise came for the Crow.

From the south side of the fortress and behind the Crow came the sound of a big-caliber rifle being fired, followed by that of a Colt .45 blast. Then a big man on a big stout stallion came over the small rise in the land with a Colt .45 in each hand, firing as fast as the gun could. The Crow were falling right and left as the big man continued to fire until both guns were empty, and then he pulled out two more and commenced firing again. Then he headed straight toward the big gate on the south side, and it opened for him to come in. Big Al and Pete met him there, and he said, "My name is Ron, and it looked as though you could use some help. I think I lightened your load some out there." They shook hands and climbed up on the wall to watch for more savages.

Then they came from behind the little knoll that Ron had come from, two hundred Crow on a full gallop toward the settlement. Arrows started flying, and bullets were fired in return. The arrows were stuck in the fortress walls without harm to anyone so far, but the Crow were taking a bad beating, with several dead braves lying on the grass beneath the walls and many more wounded.

Then came Awanatu on a full gallop toward the main gate on the south side with about twenty braves following him as fast as they could travel. When they came close to the four-foot-high stone barriers, Oh-y- Yee lunged to the left as hard as she could. Awanatu almost fell off, and before he could regain control, she lunged hard to the right and then back to the left and slid to a complete stop. He slid right up over her neck and landed hard on the ground, and then a bullet struck him in the right shoulder. Oh-y-Yee kicked him in the ribs as she ran from him, leaving him alone behind the barrier.

There were nearly thirty-five or more dead braves scattered around the perimeter of the walls, with more lying wounded and hurting so bad that they couldn't leave. That was when the other braves decided to leave, and leave they did. Awanatu was helped aboard another horse and was last seen riding west.

When the battle ended, the only being on the pasture outside the walls of the settlers' camp was a huge strong dapple-gray mare that had twisted her ankle and couldn't run away from anyone. She was free of the dreaded Awanatu finally. Now lonely and afraid, she stood motionless because she was sore all over, with some minor wounds here and there. *Have I done the right thing?* she thought as she stood there alone, wondering what would be next.

An hour and a half after the battle, when everyone was gone, Oh-y-Yee heard a sweet voice of a woman talking to her on the other side of the rock barrier. The woman appeared very pretty, tall, and slender and had kindness in her voice. She held out a carrot for Oh-y-Yee and continued to call out softly and tenderly. They felt an immediate bond, but Oh-y-Yee had not experienced that before. It was a great feeling.

The settlers were busy helping patch up their wounded, and when they finished, they started to help the Crow braves. Many of them were dead, and half the wounded had very little chance of surviving and were saying their death chants. It was not pleasant for anyone to see or hear. Pete, Big Al, Ron, and some others were all counting the dead and wounded with a total of forty-three dead and fifty-six wounded, and the rest escaped for now.

On the trail back to the Crow nation, Awanatu realized that he had made the biggest blunder of his life by not heeding the warning issued him by the Great Spirit through Slippery Fish. He asked forgiveness, and then he, by himself, crossed over to the other side to meet Slippery Fish and the Great Spirit known as God.

When all the settlers were back into camp for the evening, Pete realized he hadn't seen Anna inside the fortress. He was scared that she had been taken. The settlers opened the main gate to the south, and there stood Anna with a huge smile on her face while holding the reins of Oh-y-Yee. She told Pete that her new horse would be named Strong Mountain because she reminded Anna of a big mountain covered with rocks and snow. Oh-y-Yee was now wondering how life would change for her, but she was convinced that it would be better than before because this lady knew how to love. Pete was sure this horse would be Anna's best friend for life, and Strong Mountain would also grow to be his best friend.

The moral of the story is this: always put God first in your life and follow his commands, and all will be well with thee.

Chapter 19

It had been four months since the Crow attack upon the settlers at their settlement. Many of the events of that day were still very fresh in everyone's mind.

Today was a beautiful, bright day with the sun glowing brilliantly in the sky. There was a slight wind blowing which held the temperature lower than it really was and the grass in the meadows seemed to be waving at everything on earth. It was very impressive to see. The rye grass had a head of seeds at the top which made the waving motion seem even greater than it really was as it blew one direction and then the other. The prairie flowers had colorful flowers waving in the wind also. There was a fresh smell in the air of green grass, pollen from the grass and all of the smells of clean, fresh air from mother nature.

Out in the countryside about a mile from the camp, stood a big acorn tree, in the middle of a very pretty meadow. The tree was fairly tall with dark green leaves and a light-colored bark. It was the only tree in the entire meadow and it stood almost exactly in the center of it.

About fifty feet from the tree lay a dapple-grey horse that seemed powerful and muscled even when laying down. Oh-y-Yee was her name and she was looking intently at the acorn tree and her friend whom was sitting below it. She wondered why they had stopped here when she thought they were going for a long ride just like they had done for the last three months.

Anna Peterson was sitting under the tree in the shade trying to feel better about life in general. She was having a rough day because of her thoughts about her son Peter Jr. He had died in Iowa a few years ago and she just couldn't get over the feelings she had about him and about what had happened. Then she would always grab her locket that hung on a chain around her neck and begin to pray for help. That locket would send a sparkle up into the sky every time she fondled it.

As she sat there, she happened to look up at a low hanging branch, where a caterpillar was slowly crawling upward toward the stem of the leaf. Anna started to think about the caterpillar and his purpose in life. She then thought about the caterpillar living until it was time to spin a cocoon, which he would spin and then move into it and die. Then he would hatch out and become a beautiful butterfly. Her thoughts went to Peter Jr next while thinking about him dying, being buried and then going to heaven in a new body while still being Peter Jr. Amazing she thought. Wow, this made her feel extremely good and happy to finally understand what happened to him when he died. He was in heaven with a new beautiful body and was flying around with the greatest of ease.

Five hundred feet above the tree was the old eagle flying in the hot air above the meadow, allowing the air currents to lift and lower him because of the hot air flow coming up from the meadow down below. He was out to check on all of his friends today, when he spotted the dapple-grey horse named Oh-y-Yee lying near the tree. She was intently looking at something or someone under the tree. As he zeroed in with his eye sight, the glare of a sparkle appeared and then he found Anna sitting there holding her locket tightly. This time she looked very happy and not at all upset. The old eagle wondered what had changed her attitude from sad to very happy. Every time before when she held the locket, she appeared somber and sad. He circled several times around the tree wondering what had happened when he decided to go farther east to see what was going on in the settler's camp which had turned into a town called Centerville.

As he flew to the town of Centerville, he noticed from far off that the town had grown in size and beauty since his last visit. The log walls around the city were taller, longer and thicker than the old walls. The water canal coming from the stream was lined with nice stones and it emptied into a deep cistern for storage and when full it ran through another canal and back into the stream. The big building in the center of Centerville was even bigger than normal and now had a new color to it as it was painted a nice light brown color which blended with the surrounding colors. All of the people in the town were all busy doing their daily chores like feeding the cattle and horses, butchering, cleaning hides, weeding the garden and all of the other things that were needed to survive.

The old eagle could see Anna riding hard toward Centerville and Oh-y-Yee was loving every minute of running hard. It reminded her of her time with Awanatu which made her start thinking of him. She had very mixed emotions about him now that he was gone. One day she wished he was back with her and the next few she was glad he wasn't. Now Oh-y-Yee had a new problem and that was with Anna and Pete. She loved both of them a lot but was having trouble knowing which one was really her master. Oh- y-Yee seemed confused quite often now days.

The old eagle wondered why she was in a hurry coming back to the village. He also wondered why she was so happy after touching the locket, instead of having a sad look with crying and needing Pete to comfort her. He would watch her careful and maybe he would find out why.

Anna rode in hard, slid to a stop and dismounted and ran as fast as she could to Pete and Big Al. They were wondering what had happened that brought her in so fast and excited. She told both of them about her day while sitting under the tree and the story of the caterpillar turning into a dead caterpillar and coming back to life as a butterfly. Anna was talking so fast they could hardly keep up with her story. She said it made complete sense to her now as to what had happened to Pete Jr and it made her feel good that he now had a new body and was fine. Finally, she could continue her life in peace, thought Pete. He sure hoped this was for real and forever.

Anna had tears in her eyes while telling the story about Pete Jr and the butterfly. She was emotional spent and was shaking from the excitement. Pete and Big Al watched her walk toward their wagon with an exciting hop in her step. Pete told Al that he hoped this would a permanent change in her life and maybe then and only then they could continue being husband and wife. He had been praying for a long time that she could find peace and now maybe God had answered.

Oh-y-Yee was still wondering what had just happened when Pete came over to her and lead her toward the creek beside the city of Centerville. Pete let her drink her fill and then started to brush and wash her down. When that was finished, he led her to the meadow and turned her lose. Oh-y-Yee ran to an open spot of bare dirt and laid down and rolled through it until she was covered with dirt and dust which had caked up into her hair coat to make her look like a freshly covered wall of plaster. Soon, she ran as fast as she could toward the other horses grazing nearby. They were different than the Crow ponies in many ways. Some were work horses which were built wide, strong and built with extreme muscle densities.

There were also many mules which were weird looking horses with big nostrils and long ears. She also thought they were stubborn too. Then there were donkeys and oxen and Oh-y-Yee didn't know why the settlers even had them. There must be a reason, she thought, but what could it be? She was lonely for some of the Crow ponies, especially the good-looking young stallion. She couldn't even remember his name anymore, but she did remember he was a powerful built young male. Oh-y-Yee walked into the meadow until she reached a spot where she could be alone and think about things for a while. She laid down and was soon fast asleep.

During her deep sleep, she started to dream and dream she did. She was running through a beautiful meadow full of long rye, orchard and brome grass with many bright yellow flowers waving in the wind. The flowers all seemed to be greeting everyone and everything under God's sky above and even it seemed like they were waving to all in heaven above too. The bees were busy doing their work by going from one flower to another without even knowing they were working pollinating the flowers while gathering nectar for their food supply next winter.

In the middle of this wonderful meadow was a fast-running stream that had many smooth round rocks in it which made the water run around most of them but once in a while the water ran right over the top of them. The water running over, around and through small channels, made wonderful music which could only be heard in a fast-moving stream with many rocks trying to slow down the water. It made for a distinct music that only could be found in a stream such as this one. It sounded like a bubbling, swishing and peaceful sound that could only come from a fast-moving stream. This stream was also a home for the spawning of trout fish, which loved to go upstream to find the exact place where they were hatched and lay many eggs for the next generation. Then they would die and become food for the black bears, brown bears, grizzle bears, wolves and many other creatures of the wild.

As her dream continued, she could see more horses at the far end of the meadow near the tall beautiful Jasper pine trees. The trees seemed to go almost to the heavens above and were in outstanding colors of bright green needles, fire red bark outlined in black and big, thick and long branches that had been there for many years. Under the trees, was a herd of horses that had many different color patterns, some with solid colors and others with spots of brown, black or grey and some with white socks and a blaze down their face.

Oh-y-Yee continued her dream with the vision of a tall, strong and good-looking stallion with a blaze face and white socks on a chestnut-colored body. She was sold on his outstanding confirmation and color pattern. If she were to unite with him, what color would their offspring be? How would a dapple- grey mix with a chestnut-colored male with white socks? Humm. Was there a harem of other females around him? Did he already have a mate that he loved above all else? She would need to know before allowing her thoughts to captivate her everything.

Then her dream turned to Anna and Pete whom she had learned to love intensely, but she also missed Awanatu and his demanding ways which were not always pleasant. But she missed him anyway. Pete and Anna were very nice but somewhat simple without excitement. Oh-y-Yee really wanted something exciting or maybe a family.

Just then she was startled by a loud booming sound that made the earth shake below her feet. Then came a heavy rainfall which was very warm and soothing in most ways. Oh-y-Yee jumped to her feet and started toward the settler's town of Centerville. By the time she arrived the path was turning to mud which was slippery and tiring for her. It also made the trip much more time consuming. She arrived at Centerville just before dark and was still thinking about the dream of all dreams. Soon, she heard Anna's voice asking where she had been and why she was gone so long. Oh-y-Yee loved Anna's sweet and soft voice when she was showing kindness. Pete arrived and was concerned about the welfare of Oh-y-Yee but in a different tone than Anna's voice. They took Oh-y-Yee to the center of town and put her into the livery stable, rubbed her down and gave her some oats followed by a nice helping of timothy hay. She loved this attention. Oh-y-Yee knew she was loved deeply by both Anna and Pete, but something was missing. She would sleep good tonight and that she did.

Morning came with a beautiful sunrise in the east with a small group of clouds mingling in and out of view of the people and animals below. There was a slight wind blowing from the south, southeast which if it continued would most likely bring rainfall.

Oh-y-Yee was up and about out in the meadow again when she begins to think about the dream from yesterday. She wondered if there was a big stallion in this part of the world, and if so, where was he? All that she could do is to wait and see if he appeared somewhere or sometime. When he does come, she hoped she would not be disappointed in him or what he meant to her. Time would tell.

Centerville was busy today with everyone doing their part in the town. Some were hunting, some gathering firewood, some making the morning meal and the children were running and playing as always. The young boys were down by the stream fishing and hoping for the "big one" to bite the hook and get reeled in to make a fine meal later. Others were busy cleaning the homes, wagons and preparing to build another home in the city for the Olson's. They had made a new home for someone in the settlement about every two months and it was looking more and more like the town they left in Iowa.

Around noon Anna walked over to Pete and Big Al and asked where Oh-y-Yee was and they shrugged their shoulders and muttered, don't know. Then they talked about the last time they had seen her and they all agreed the last time was when she was walking toward the meadow early this morning. Anna thought they should go looking for her and both men started laughing while saying she will be home later when she lacks food or companionship.

The old eagle was out today catching the early air currents as they lifted him upward and then just as fast shoved him down toward the ground. He always enjoyed the old hot air currents or the lack of them completely to give him a free ride up and down for several miles at a time. While air surfing, he noticed Oh-y-Yee was 7 miles south of Centerville walking toward the mountains to the south. That was puzzling to the old eagle. Why was she out here all alone heading toward the mountains that had hardly ever been ridden by the settlers. He noticed she continued into the brush around the edge of the meadow and then disappeared into the thickets. Why is she doing this thought the old eagle as he flew overhead.

Oh-y-Yee didn't know why she was there either, but something was pulling her toward the highest mountain on the south side. There was a smell in the air that attracted her to continue farther on toward that odor. She wasn't sure what it was but it attracted her more and more as the smell intensified. She continued on well after the sun set in the west. Then Oh-y-Yee laid down and soon fell asleep.

In Centerville, Anna, Pete, Big Al and almost everyone else wondered where Oh-y-Yee had gone. Was she out in the prairie lying injured or did a pack of wolves or a mountain lion get her? Anna was worried but the men just shrugged it off like it wasn't a big deal.

Oh-y-Yee had fallen asleep and then her dream started up again. She could see the band of wild horses out in the meadow running, kicking their legs in the air while some were content to just munch on the new grass beneath their feet. The horses were of many colors, different ages both male and female.

They all belonged to the herd and acted as one big family. The little colts were running as fast as they could one direction, then turn on a dime and go the other direction faster than before. They would race each other in big, wide circles and then go full blast the opposite direction while kicking their rear legs high in the air. Oh-y-Yee was now dreaming of her days as a young colt racing back and forth as though it was yesterday. She was always the fastest, strongest and best-looking female in the group and she knew it, too. The dapple-gray color was always different than all the other horses and that made her feel special.

The dream continued on about her life until it was interrupted by this urge to figure out who this stallion was that appeared in her dream. Oh-y-Yee was bothered by the thoughts of this big, strong and powerful male that had entered her life. He was massive and good looking as well.

Oh-y-Yee slept all night and awakened at sunrise the next morning. During the night the clouds had blown away leaving a clear sky which in turn made it very cold this morning. It sent a chill down her spine all the way to her feet.

Oh-y-Yee started walking through the brush and bushes which were on a hillside within five miles of the base the mountains to the south of Centerville. The land had a slight incline upward toward the foot of the mountains. She was now in the part of the foothills that had small clearings here and there the size of a city block.

The old eagle was flying around checking on his friends today when he flew over the city of Centerville. He noticed the glimmer or sparkle of light flashing upward that was coming up from down below. He noticed that it came from Anna's necklace which held the locket with the little diamond on it and a picture of Pete junior inside of it. He knew that something was wrong down below. But what could it be, he wondered as he flew around in circles, high up in the sky? He was unnoticed and was allowing the air currents to lift him one moment and let him free fall the next. This kind of flying he enjoyed most of all.

The old eagle headed west to see how the Crow Indians were doing and, on the way, he would fly over the mountains to the south to see what Ron was doing.

Now he was flying high in the sky over the area of Ron's cave and his home inside of the cave. There was no sign of Ron or his horse as the old eagle flew overhead. He wondered, "where is Ron and what is he doing?" The old bird started to fly in big circles spreading out further each time he went around the circle. He could cover a vast area simply by doing the circles and extending the size each time around.

After an hour of the circles, he landed on the limb of a large Jasper pine tree. It reminded him of his home. There he rested and dozed off into a deep sleep. It lasted for over an hour.

In the meantime, Oh-y-Yee was walking higher and higher into the foothills of the mountains to the south of Centerville. She would stop to graze on the lush new grass in the small meadows and then continue on through the bushes and into another meadow, where she would also graze for a few minutes and then move on. The grass was young, tender and tasted great.

The old eagle was flying about again high up in the sky while allowing the air currents lift and lower him for no reason at all. He totally enjoyed this type of flying. He also enjoyed the fact that he could see for miles around him and admire God's handy work. "It was all so beautiful." He murmured out loud.

There was no sign of Ron or his horses down below as the old eagle had been searching more intensely now than before. "Where could he be?" the old eagle said out loud as he continued to look below.

Ron was twenty miles to the east of his cave hunting for elk or deer with little or no luck at all. He had been out here for nearly three and a half days and had not even seen a deer or an elk. Where could they be, he wondered as he started up the side of the mountain where there were many larger meadows with wonderful grass. Maybe he would have better luck there in finding large game. Ron's horse, Shadow was getting tired of the climb up the side of the mountains, just to find another one to climb.

Ron was not about to give up so they continued upward toward the high meadows at 6,000 feet above sea level.

Back at Centerville, everyone was aware of the fact that Oh-y-Yee was missing. Anna, Pete and big Al were more worried than they were letting on to the others. All Anna could think of was Oh-y-Yee and her welfare. She was wondering if a pack of wolves cornered her or a bear or if she had slipped a fallen over a cliff. Anna was wondering if Pete and some of the men could follow the trail left by Oh-y-Yee to find her. Pete replied that the trail was too old to do any tracking. They would have to wait a few days or go now on a scouting mission, hoping to find her which would be like looking for a needle in a haystack.

Oh-y-Yee was heading eastward while slowing gaining in altitude on the sides of the mountain. The meadows were beautiful this time of the year. The grass was waving in the wind, changing the colors depending on whether it was blowing to or from Oh-y-Yee. Dark blue with the wind from one direction and light green when it came back toward her. The wild flowers had dark green stems with an arrangement of white, blue, red and yellow flowers which were also blowing in the wind making the meadow look unbelievably beautiful. She continued on up over a small hill in the meadow and to her surprise, she recognized the area below her about 50 feet. It was the Crow Indian burial grounds where she had been many times before. She wandered in and around the grave sites being careful not to bump into the lodge poles that held the lifeless body of someone ten feet above the ground to protect them from harm. Then she spotted a familiar grave site which belonged to a great chieftain and a friend of hers, Slippery Fish.

Oh-y-Yee laid down at the edge of the burial grounds and fell into a deep sleep. She started to dream and dream she did! Here was Slippery Fish walking toward her with his hand held out toward her with something orange in color in his palm. He kept on talking in his smooth and wonderful sounding voice about nice girl, nice girl, come here sweetie. Oh-y-Yee thought he was the nicest man she had ever known. His erect stature, stately looks and strong body made him very good looking, thought Oh-y-Yee. Soon, he was petting her head and she was eating from the palm of his hand. It was good tasting and Slippery Fish called them carrots. "He was very nice." exclaimed Oh-y-Yee.

Her dream continued on with a man yelling at her and he was mad. It was Awanatu. He wanted her to run faster than before and for a longer period of time, like when they were preparing for war. She wanted to run from him but was somewhat afraid to do so. Then a group of Crow braves gathered around her and Awanatu and he mellowed out and became somewhat tolerable. Soon the entire camp of men, women and children were there watching the disturbance. Suddenly, she awoke and was wondering where and why that dream had entered her mind. Strange, she thought as she stood up and stretched her body out as far as she could. That always felt great when one's muscles had been in one position so long.

Oh-y-Yee did not know why or how come she was wandering the side of the mountain south of Centerville but something was just pulling her in that direction. It was a strange feeling that she could not explain. Now she started walking more toward the south which would take her higher up into the mountains away from the small meadows toward the pine trees. After two hours of walking, she reached the edge of the meadow where the Jasper pine trees had started to grow upward since the beginning of the earth. Oh-y-Yee stopped to catch her breath and turned to look back where she had come from. It was breath taking to see. The hillside below looked much steeper and bigger than it appeared on the way up. The colors were down right gorgeous! Down below were beautiful meadows covered in green and blueish colored grass, large and small rocks of different colors, many different colored flowers along with streams of clear water running in zig and zag directions down the hills and mountain side. There were also small ponds where the land leveled out with beaver dams holding back more water than normal to make it deep enough to offer them protection from their enemies. The whole picture was of God's handiwork and it was incomparable to anything ever made by man.

Oh-y-Yee laid down under one of the first Jasper Pines she came to at the edge of the tree line by the last meadow she crossed. It was beautiful looking out over and down the mountain side while seeing the valley below. Soon, she was sound asleep again.

The old eagle was flying in larger circles all the time looking intensely toward the ground looking for signs of Ron or Oh-y-Yee. He was tired now and was thinking of finding a large Jasper Pine tree to spend the night in and on a large branch. He wondered, where could Ron be?

Back at Centerville, everyone was now more than worried about Oh-y-Yee, the dapple-gray mare, they had grown quite fond of. Where was she, what had happened, why did she leave them and many other questions as well. The questions would all be answered in the next few days, they hoped.

Ron was also bedding down for the night. He had finally shot and killed a large bull Elk and had butchered the animal, packed the meat on pack horses and would be ready to leave for his cave early tomorrow morning. He would sleep well tonight after a hard day's work plus a belly full of Elk steak. Soon he was fast asleep, snoring like a train pulling a heavy load up the side of a steep hill.

800 miles west of the mountains south of Centerville was the Crow Indian camp. They were working harder than before the war with the settlers, due to the fact they lost so many young braves in the fight. Now, boys and women had to take over and perform some of the duties the braves had performed previously. Soon, it would be time to turn in for the night here also and tomorrow would be another day of hard work for everyone. They all agreed that Awanatu had acted hastily when he decided to attack the settlers at Centerville. He should have heeded the warning from Slippery Fish in his dream from the great Spirit, instead of rushing the attack out of anger, they all thought. Now all of the women, children and braves were working hard every day just to survive instead of having time for parties and dancing. Not only did they lose young men, but also many horses and weapons that would need to be replaced. It was a huge mistake on his part. Soon, they too were all asleep for the night.

Morning came with a beautiful sun rise, warm weather, not a cloud in the sky and a slight breeze from the southwest. It was a perfect day weather wise.

The settlers in Centerville were up early today working away at the everyday chores. Ole was working with several of the men as they were preparing to go hunting for deer or elk in the south mountains.

They very seldom hunted there, but this time they had another reason to go there as well. They would be looking to find or trying to track Oh-y-Yee, just so Pete and Anna would feel better. Ole hoped they could find her but he wasn't very positive about it either. He had six men with him as well as 6 extra pack horses for the meat they would need to haul home. Soon, they started out across the big meadow to the south of Centerville, past the big lonely tree standing in the middle of the meadow. Ole and the men were heading toward a break in the briar bushes near the foot of the mountains where they could pick up an old game trail which headed around and upward toward the big meadows that lie ahead. This was a slow-moving group with so many horses and a couple of them carrying their campsite equipment.

The old eagle was out flying around the southern mountains this morning looking for the news from down below when he spotted Ron, Shadow and a couple of pack horses loaded with what appeared to be elk meat. The smell that came up from below to the old eagle verified the fact that it was elk meat. Birds like this old eagle had unbelievable eye sight and a keen sense of smell. Ron was headed west ward toward his cave 25 miles away and it was slow going with the heavy load of elk meat. He would have a lot of work to do tonight when they arrived back at the cave, thought Ron, as he rode slowly along an old game trail. Rub down the horses would take time, then feed them some wild oats and turn them out into the meadow. Next, he would have to clean the equipment and put it away properly or it would become stiff and out of shape. Then he would call it a day. Tomorrow the hard work would start with the cutting of the meat into proper sizes and then curing it over the campfire slowly. This would make jerky that would last for many months without spoiling.

Oh-y-Yee was moving slightly uphill while grazing on the side of the high mountain meadow. She was eating the good, young rye, orchard and brome grasses for her breakfast this morning. Her belly would soon be full and then she would lie down and rest while her stomach digested all of it. Life was really good, she thought, as she continued to eat. After thirty minutes she found a nice level area to rest on under the shade of a big Jasper pine tree.

After a few minutes, Oh-y-Yee was fast asleep and dreaming again. This time her dream was all about the attack on the settlers with Awanatu riding her very hard for days before the attack and how her anger was mounting to the point of deciding to get rid of him once and for all. In her dream she laughed when she dislodged him from her back and laughed even louder when he was injured badly. It was great to see after all of the mistreatment he had given her. Then she remembered how this special lady they called Anna came to her after the conflict with loving kindness. Anna had rubbed her head, patted her neck while speaking softly in her ear. Then Anna took her to the fortress where she met Pete and Big Al. They too were very kind and gentle. She loved all of them, but now she was confused because she was running from them up into the mountains. Why? How come? All she could think of was the pulling at her heart that was taking her here. Why? She didn't know. After about an hour Oh-y-Yee was up and heading up the old game trail toward the peaks of the mountains.

As the old eagle was flying around in the big circles, he noticed Oh-y-Yee climbing upward on the side of the mountain. What was she doing here, he wondered? She was a long way from Centerville. This was very puzzling to the old eagle. Soon he landed on a big branch of a nearby pine tree to rest for a while. Stopping more often to rest was becoming quite common now for him as he was nearly eighteen years old. He would just watch Oh-y-Yee for a while to see where she was going. Time would tell, he thought as he too dozed off for a while. When he awakened, Oh-y-Yee was gone and to where he knew not. Now he started flying around in circles again trying to spot her. He could not find her in the first half hour of flying, so he decided to fly toward Ron's cave to see what was going on there. On the way to the cave, he became very tired and decided to land in a tree for a short nap. He did land soon and quickly fell asleep. He was so tired he slept all night long and at dawn he was awakened by the howling of a wolf pack as they were greeting each other. The birds were singing and flying from tree to tree enjoying another day that God had given them.

Ole and the hunters from Centerville had reached an area that looked very good for hunting elk and deer. Hoof prints were scattered all around the edges of the high mountain meadows and signs were in the tall grass that showed where teeth had bitten off the upper portions of the best grasses. Soon, they found several elk drinking from a small pool of water at the edge of one of the small meadows. They crawled toward them and on Ole's command they fired, killing four big male elk. Now the work would begin, thought Ole. And it did. They worked very hard to bleed them out, skin all of them and remove the inner organs quickly to prevent spoilage of the meat. Then they began to cut the meat into roasts, steaks and jerky strips. This would take the rest of the day so they would camp overnight here and then head back to Centerville tomorrow. They had not even saw a sign of Oh-y-Yee's hoof prints or any horse manure either. Where could she have gone and why, wondered Ole as he worked?

In Centerville Anna was holding her locket, which was on her necklace, while she was praying again and asking God to bring the joy of her life back to her. She missed Oh-y-Yee so much she could hardly control her emotions. Pete also missed her a lot along with everyone in Centerville. All of them wondered what could have happened to make Oh-y-Yee leave them and especially go to the south mountains. They didn't think they would ever find the answer to that question.

Night fall had come again and the night had become very silent. You could hear the wolves howling far off in the distance, a coyote calling for his mate and wild animals grazing in the big meadow near Centerville. The great smell of nature was in the air and one could hear the water running down the stream, around and over the rocks making its own sound, similar to music of a full orchestra. Oh-y-Yee had laid down to rest as the Sun went down on the other side of the mountains and soon, she was fast asleep and dreaming. She heard the sounds of the water running down the stream while running over, around and between the rocks making a beautiful sound that was peaceful in nature. With it was carried an aroma of pure cleanliness which matched the clear, clean water that was racing downward toward the larger stream, which would then lead it to another one and continue until it reached the river down below in the valley.

Oh-y-Yee continued to dream on in amazement with the beauty that was here on earth and in the heavens above. She was sure that anyone who had seen this countryside, would credit God for the many wonderful things He had made and did it with only a command from His voice. Like the stars in the sky which had been named and numbered each with its own identity. There were millions of them and she knew they were named and numbered. How could God remember each one by name and also by their number. Unbelievable she thought.

Her mind wandered off to the deer, elk and antelope. How did God give them the knowledge of knowing when to have babies, when to grow long hair to protect from the long and cold winters? How did they know when to shed the extra hair so they could enjoy the summer without being too hot for comfort?

Every year they had the young at the same exact time, all being born in a period of just a few days. Her mind wandered to the fish in the streams which returned to their birth place every year to lay eggs in the same location as they were hatched for the next generation to hatch. Then the mature fish would die after completing the egg laying and float downstream only to become food for the bears, wolves and birds of the air. How did God know how many eggs would be needed to hatch in order to keep the correct number of fishes in the streams without under or over population of each type? How did He make the trout mate with only the trout and not the catfish? How many extras were hatched just to be food for their predators? How did God keep every fish, bird and land animal to only mate with his or her own kind in order to keep many different animals into their own families without becoming one mixed group?

Only God had that answer, thought Oh-y-Yee as she slept on, while dreaming some more. This time it was about horses and donkeys. Why could a horse mate with a donkey producing a mule. So, God made the mule so they could not reproduce because then we would only have mules and be without horses and donkeys. God has a plan that is way beyond our ability to understand and comprehend thought Oh- y-Yee. Everything was super well planned and each animal group had many things that needed to be controlled. The number born, the number that would die before they reached adulthood, the number that were there just to be food for another group of predators as well as the amount of food available for them to grow on and to continue to thrive. Plus, many more things that we don't even know about. Wow!

The next morning Oh-y-Yee was slow and tired. She remembered every part of her dream and thanked God for revealing it all to her in the dream last night.

Today was a beautiful sunny day with the temperature nearly perfect without a cloud in the sky. Ole and the hunters had returned to Centerville from the south side mountains with the four large elk, all butchered and cut into steaks, roast and other nice cuts of meat. The people of Centerville were all gathering around them to see how much meat they had brought back from the mountains to the south. Anna came at a dead gallop to where everyone was gathered to talk to the men of the hunting party.

Hopefully she would hear news about Oh-y-Yee from Ole or some of the other men in the hunting party. Soon, she was told that they had not seen any sign of Oh-y-Yee or any other horse. Anna was devastated by the news. Ole stated that maybe she had wandered back to the Crow Indian camp where she was familiar with everyone and maybe lonesome, too. With that comment, Anna turned and ran back toward her little cabin with tears running down her face and her heart broken.

It was a beautiful day to be soaring through the air allowing the wind currents from down below to push you higher and higher until the current changed and dropped hundreds of feet in just a few seconds.

The old eagle was out checking on all of the people he knew and today he was starting at the Crow Indian camp to see what was happening there. A couple of hours later he reached the camp and started flying around it in big circles while checking on the Crow people. The children were playing in a small creek nearby, laughing and running while pretending to be hunters or warriors. They were using all of their energy and soon they would be very tired.

The women of the camp were doing their daily chores, roasting meat, making jerky or boiling soups for later in the day from meats that could not be smoked or cured for later. Some of the women were down by the stream washing the clothing, others were collecting water from the stream for drinking later.

Some were sewing new buckskins, some making needles from bones and some of them gathering firewood.

The old eagle noticed the men were gone from the camp. He wondered if they were hunting for game for food or were, they planning an attack on another group of Indians or settlers. Time would tell he thought as he widened his circle to see if he could spot dust rising up from the forest floor anywhere around the camp. He continued making wide circles high in the sky while looking down below for the braves from the Crow camp. Twenty-two miles to the east, he found them skinning a couple of buffalo.

They were excited about getting two big bulls which would supply them with a lot of jerky and smoked meats for later days.

The old eagle continued to the east now toward the southern mountains to see if he could find Ron or Oh-y-Yee. It would take the rest of the day to get there so he would find a large tree near Ron's cave to roost in for the night.

This morning was very bright with beautiful sunshine and only a few clouds high up in the clear blue sky. This morning, Oh-y-Yee was moving higher in the mountains while grazing on new lush grass. It was a great day to be out in God's earth she thought as she continued to graze on the rye and orchard grass. Something was pulling her upward toward the mountain tops close the point where the tree line stopped and the snow began. Every once in a while, she would stop, raise her head higher in the air and suck in a deep breath as though she was searching for a certain smell or odor. Oh-y-Yee was confused by this behavior as it was new to her. She continued onward and upward. Oh-y-Yee for no reason at all, whinnied fairly loud and miles away she heard an answering whinny. This sparked her interest and set her mind in motion. Who did that whinny belong to, a male or a female and where did it come from?

The east, west or the north or was it much closer? She was moving toward the sound now at a pace that was much faster than before.

The sounds of the whinny traveled farther and faster this morning because of the clear sky and of the early hour of the day. As the forest and meadows became buzzling with animals grazing, running or just moving through the tall grass, the noises would increase dramatically.

25 miles from Oh-y-Yee, stood a tall, strong and good-looking stallion that had heard and answered the whinny with his own deep, powerful voice. He was chestnut colored with a blaze down the middle of his face. The mane and tail were colored much darker than the chestnut hair on his body, more of a walnut color. It made him look much better than if he was the same color overall. He too was excited to hear another horse whinny this high up in the mountains, especially one that he did not know. Who? Where? Why was another horse this high up into the mountains? This stallion wanted to run toward the whinny but he couldn't because he was tethered in his master's meadow near the top of the mountain by a steep cliff which the Crow Indians had named Skull Cap. It received its name

because of the steep granite cliff that went straight up toward the sky. To the Crow, this mountain was very sacred because of the skull cap look but with a hidden cave which looked like an eye socket. They believed that anyone who lived there was a ghost of the Great Spirit. They would travel by it by a distance of at least five miles so they would not wake the gods of the Great Spirit.

The old eagle was flying around the southern mountains now looking or snooping around to find out who was up and about this morning. He was sure he could find Oh-y-Yee and maybe even Ron, although he was always hidden very well. He was flying at the 7,000-foot level of the mountain when he spotted a pack of wolves stalking a large old and wounded bull elk. It would be a fairly easy kill for the pack, even if it was daytime.

A few minutes later, the elk was becoming breakfast for the pack of hungry wolves. They would devour all they could eat and the balance of the old bull would be food for the lesser predators of the forest. When they were finished, the vultures would finish the cleanup. They were God's janitors.

Oh-y-Yee continued traveling toward the sound of the whinny of another horse. Her mind was running at full speed while wondering if the other horse was a male or a female. She thought it sounded like a large, strong and powerful stallion. She hurried onward excitedly.

Tonight, she laid down and was fast asleep quickly and just as fast she started dreaming again about the big stallion she had thought about a few days before. The dream lasted all night long and she was confused as to why this same dream continued nightly.

In the morning she awakened when the sun came up over the small cliff just to the south of her. Oh-y- Yee was stiff and sore and felt very tired. Then she heard the whinny again and instantly she was wide awake and heading toward the sound of the whinny. Traveling faster than ever and sometimes running like she did when she was with the Crow Indians. Every few minutes, she would stop, whinny and listen until she heard the reply from the other horse. Now they were closer together and she knew he was a stallion. He sounded big and strong. She continued upward on the mountain side, stopping every few minutes to listen for the stallion's whinny again. This was very exciting she thought and she hurried toward the sound of the last whinny.

Suddenly as she rounded a corner by a large stone cliff and came face to face with a big, strong and good-looking stallion. They stopped suddenly and started to stare at each other intently. Oh-y-Yee was intrigued by his size, muscling and over all great confirmation. The big stallion was also very impressed with her overall confirmation and extreme muscling throughout her entire body. He hadn't ever seen a female that was as strong and as big as Oh-y-Yee. She started flirting with the stallion doing silly little side dances, nipping at his rump and shoulders in a playful manner. He wasn't sure how to receive this flirting but he tried to follow the lead. This continued on for several minute when suddenly Oh-y-Yee bit him in the rump, turned and ran as fast as she could away from him. He was surprised but recovered quickly and started to race after she as fast as he could run. The stallion was surprised with the speed Oh-y-Yee's running speed and amazed at her ability to cut sharp corners without slipping or falling. They raced around the little meadow all afternoon and well into the night.

The next morning the old eagle was flying around the mountain looking downward trying to find Oh-y- Yee when he spotted her in a meadow down below. He was surprised when he realized that she had a friend with her, a stallion. He soon realized that the two horses below were infatuated with each other to the point that they didn't even notice the events around them. Oh-y-Yee was dancing and prancing all around the big stallion in a real flirting way by zig-zagging back and forth in front him one moment and behind him the next.

The old eagle left the tree he was sitting while watching the two lovers below as he started flying eastward and slightly south. He was looking for Ron now.

At the settler town, Pete, Anna and big Al were setting around the dinner table talking when Anna blurted out, "I wonder where Oh-y-Yee is tonight." Pete and Big Al looked at her as if to expect her to start crying but enough time had passed so she could now control her emotions better than before. They talked for what seemed like hours about the possible places that Oh-y-Yee could be or have gone.

Anna thought she probably went back to the Crow Indians; Pete thought another wagon train or horse traders had taken her but Big Al said she probably turned stupid and starting looking for a mate. Both Anna and Pete abruptly turned their look to Big Al in disgust. Anna because of the stupid remark and Pete because couldn't see Oh-y-Yee as a family girl.

Several days had passed since Oh-y-Yee had found the big stallion and they had the greatest time of their lives running around flirting and dancing sideways, forward and backwards. They were lost in love for each other.

Ron had been gone for several days exploring the mountainside near his cave when he arrived back at the cave's entrance tonight. It was dark out so he went directly into the cave and started a fire and was soon digging out some potatoes from the sand box in the corner of the cave as well as some beef jerky for the evening meal. After eating he became very tired and fell sound asleep.

The next morning Ron was up early to do his chores and check on his big stallion and the two other mares that he had left at home. An hour later when Ron found the two mares, he also found the hobbles on the ground that had been on the stallion. The stallion was missing. He was disgusted because now he would have to spend time tracking the stallion until he found him. And that could take days if he wasn't lucky.

Two miles away on the mountainside, Oh-y-Yee and the stallion were enjoying grazing in a small meadow near a stream of spring water flowed downhill rapidly. The water would flow into the rocks making perfect music and round the rocks making different sound of music, a softer and sweeter sound. The wind was also blowing through the meadow making the flowers rock from side to side like they were dancing in perfect unison with their many colors flowing back and forth like a moving rainbow. It was gorgeous to behold.

Ron was riding his old mare through the mountain side following the trail of his stallion when he came upon another set of hoof prints on the ground. He was surprised as he wasn't aware of another horse being this high up in the mountains where no one lived and very few ever even came up this high. He continued on reading the trail below his horse trying to figure out where they were headed. Soon he would have to pull off of the trail and make camp for the night.

The old eagle was flying overhead when he spotted Ron and his mare down below. He was wondering what they were doing way over here instead of staying in the cave at the top of Skull Cap Mountain. Something must be wrong he thought as he landed on a large branch to stay for the night. Tomorrow would take care of the things of itself he thought as he dozed off to sleep.

The next morning the sky was covered in low hanging clouds that contained rain within. It was almost like a low fog making visibility seem like it was midnight. The ground was wet which made Ron wonder how much rain had come down during the night. He was hoping it wasn't a lot because if it was a heavy rainfall, the mountain streams would most likely be impossible to cross until tomorrow. He had already ridden through several streams which would block him from returning home to the Skull Cap cave and he wasn't prepared to stay out on the mountain side tonight. It could be a very long and cold night he thought as he continued riding and following the hoof prints on the forest floor. It was getting harder to find the hoof prints now than it was ten minutes ago which meant it had rained more here than it did several miles behind him. Ron came to an opening into a meadow where he realized the mountain stream on the other side of the meadow was overflowing and streaming wildly down the mountainside with the sound of several freight trains. It was very loud as the water had tremendous force which was uprooting trees and slamming them into the rocks and in one spot the trees had piled up and was damming the water behind it. Ron knew that soon the force of thousands of gallons of water behind the blockade, would break open a pathway through the log jam and then race at hundreds of feet per second toward the valley below causing even more destruction along the stream. He decided to go to higher ground and find a place to camp for the night where he would be safe from the rushing water.

Ron found a nice place in the middle of a group of cedar trees on the top of a knoll in the center of the meadow. He would cut some branches and then make a bed, then hunt for some quail or a rabbit or two. Ron was busy for several hours gathering firewood and getting a couple of quail ready for the campfire. Soon he ate well and turned in for the night.

The big stallion and Oh-y-Yee hardly even noticed the heavy down pour of rain as they continued flirting with each other but soon they to laid down to sleep. They were tired.

The next morning the big old bald eagle was flying around looking for Ron and the stallion again. Soon he noticed Ron's camp in the center of a bunch of cedar trees and thought he had better stay there another day as the mountain stream was now very wide with wildly rushing water going toward the valley floor at what seemed to be one hundred miles per hour. About four miles from Ron, the old eagle spotted the two horses grazing in the meadow down below. He noticed the flirting had slowed down and they were content just to graze on the lush orchard grass on the meadows floor. Interesting he thought!

Three days later Ron felt safe to proceed looking for his big chestnut colored stallion so after an early breakfast he started out in the same direction as before. But it was slow going now as the hoof prints were no longer visible to the naked eye. He was just trying to think of the most likely place a stallion would go after leaving his home meadow. He remembered the stallion always liked thickets of berry plants because it could keep the flies off of him while he ate the very tasty berries. Ron decided to check out each berry patch he found until he found the stallion. He was wondering why the big strong stallion would wander away from the cave but he couldn't think of one reason as to why he would do that.

Back at the little town in the eastern end of the valley, Pete and Anna along with Big Al had given up hope of ever seeing Oh-y-Yee again. They wondered many times as to what might have happened and each time they came up with a new reason as to what happened.

Two mornings later, Ron rounded a corner and there was a large berry patch so he started checking it out when his horse whinnied. They stopped instantly and there it was, a returned whinny that belonged to his stallion. Ron raced forward toward the patch when his stallion appeared out of the south side.

Ron quickly roped the stallion and reeled him into the horse he was riding. Then he noticed a big dapple- grey mare come out of the patch as well. She was stunning with very good muscling throughout her body. He wanted this mare so he tied the stallion to a tree and rode after the mare thinking he could rope her as well and bring her home with them. But, to his surprise the mare was very fast and has extremely quick turns the right or the left. Then she raced straight down the mountain side with blazing speed. His horse no match for her so he pulled up and stopped. The last thing he seen of Oh-y-Yee was dirt flying up from her feet and her tail in the air and she was gone down the mountainside.

Ron turned his horse around and went back to where he had tied the stallion. He tied the lead rope around his saddle horn and proceeded to go back to the cave called Skull Cap. It took four days to complete the trip homeward. All that time Ron was thinking about the big, strong and beautiful mare that he had seen back by the berry patch. That's all the stallion could think about also.

Five months ago, Oh-y-Yee had left the settlers little town and now she found herself on the valley floor ten miles from the town. She was going home and was thinking of Pete and Anna and she increased the speed of her walk from the exciting thought of being able to see them again. She grazed in the meadow today and was afraid that the towns people would not be happy to see her and later she laid down to sleep for the night.

Early the next morning she was up and found her foot steps were increasing in speed and when she was a mile from the town, she broke into a full running gallop. A sentry at the city wall was the first to see her and he sounded an alarm of an incoming horse. All of the people were running toward the sentry trying to see if it was an Indian attack or some wild horse that was being chased by wolves.

Anna and Pete arrived just about the same time the horse reached the town's wall when Anna realized it was Oh-y-Yee who was now named Strong Mountain. She let out a scream and ran through the gateway to greet her. Anna was crying and rubbing all over Oh-y-Yee's neck when Peter caught up with Anna.

Anna and Pete were so excited and happy to see Oh-y-Yee that they didn't even notice that 45 settlers were watching them rub her all over her body. The crowd clapped their hands and shouted they should have a party to celebrate. The party lasted until the early morning hours and then Anna put Oh-y-Yee into the newly constructed stable. She fed her some top rye grass hay and went to her cabin. There she couldn't go to sleep for several hours from the excitement of the evening.

Happiness filled the camp for many days as everyone took their turn in brushing the beautiful filly. Oh-y- Yee was the happiest horse in the entire camp and was treated like the Queen that she was.

Several months passed and things had gone back to normal for Pete, Anna and Big Al and the entire group of settlers. Hunting was always happening, gathering firewood and water continued and life in general was sailing along smoothly.

It was time for winter to come but it was coming later this year than normal as tomorrow would be Christmas day.

Early the next morning everyone woke up to a large snow storm which had dumped 5 inches of new snow making the entire camp look very clean. The children were excitedly running and playing in the new snow while most of the adults were digging themselves out of the snowfall. It was hard work and they were very busy. Anna didn't have time to go to the stable until after 2 pm. She had to shovel a huge pile of snow from in front of the door in order to open it. When she finally opened the door and went inside, she screamed with excitement so loud that most of the settlers came running to the stable thinking that Anna had been hurt badly.

When they arrived inside the stable, they found Anna hugging Oh-y-Yee and screaming with tears running down her face. The settlers were wondering why Anna was screaming so loudly when they noticed a cute little colt laying in the deep straw in the corner of the stall. They wanted Anna to get the colt up so they could see if she had her mothers beautiful confirmation and colors.

Anna got the colt to stand up and it had outstanding confirmation, maybe even better than her mother. Her color was a beautiful light brown dotted with little white spots and a long solid black mane and tail. She was even prettier than her mother and jumped and kicked in the air just like her sassy mother.

Anna named the gorgeous little filly "Snow Flake." To this day Oh-y-Yee and Snow Flake can be found running in the meadows around Centerville enjoying their friends and freedom forever.

www.ingramcontent.com/pod-product-compliance
Lightning Source LLC
Chambersburg PA
CBHW060800210726
48292CB00013B/1512